THE
OTHER
BOOK

THE
OTHER
BOOK

Philip Womack

BLOOMSBURY

First published in Great Britain in 2008 by Bloomsbury Publishing Plc
36 Soho Square, London, W1D 3QY

Lines from the poem 'Death & Co.' by Sylvia Plath, are from *Sylvia Plath:
Collected Poems* by Sylvia Plath, Faber and Faber Ltd, 1981

A CIP catalogue record of this book is available from the British Library

ISBN 978 0 7475 9043 9

All papers used by Bloomsbury Publishing are natural, recyclable products
made from wood grown in well-managed forests. The manufacturing processes
conform to the environmental regulations of the country of origin.

Typeset by Dorchester Typesetting Group Ltd
Printed in Great Britain by Clays Ltd, St Ives Plc

1 3 5 7 9 10 8 6 4 2

www.bloomsbury.com

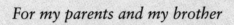

For my parents and my brother

One

ain exploded in the middle of the boy's stomach. It burned briefly, red-hot, and all the breath went out of him. He smashed into a wall and banged his head; eerie shapes danced before his eyes, and then he felt nothing.

When he came to, the boy looked warily around him. What had once been his father was still standing in the middle of Great Hall. Little light could squeeze its way through the grimy glass of the windows. The boy shrank further into the corner where he had been thrown. The Hall was full of smoke that rolled in black billows. The portraits on the walls had long ago been covered in soot. His eyes were stinging unpleasantly. He rubbed them slowly, and blinked three or four times.

He remembered how it had been before *it* had

happened and his young life had been changed beyond all recognition. If he'd been standing in Great Hall in the sunlight, the stained glass of his father's coat of arms would make plays of colour on his hands – startling, blood-coloured reds, deep, sea-green blues, and vivid golds. He'd known the heraldic names for the colours, and had loved their strange syllables – *gules* for red, *sable* for black, *azure* for blue. But now everything was the same dull, dirty shade. His father's glory had been coated over. The heralds had no word for that colour.

He held out his hands in front of him. They were covered in blood.

Huge oak logs crackled and spat in the vast fireplace, which was carved with the coats of arms of his ancestors. His dogs were huddled nearby, yelping and scuffling, their hackles raised, their little fangs bared. Proud Fairfax and sweet Blanche were doing their best to protect him. They crouched at the ready, but there was nothing they could do. What was facing him now was worse than anything they ever met on their rambles in the woods and fields around Oldstone Manor. They were barely older than puppies, had never killed more than a bird.

The boy touched his stomach carefully. It was whole. He had not been wounded. The blood was not his own.

He saw Jemima, his old nurse, standing in the doorway. Her white apron, always the brightest thing in his life, was blackened and torn. She was almost bent double. 'Fly! Fly!' she was shrieking at him in her cracked, quavery voice, but the boy couldn't.

He couldn't dare, because then he would have to run past the thing that had once been his father, which now stood in the centre of Great Hall, so drenched in blood that his clothes stuck to his body, grinning, revealing his decaying teeth, his sword ready for the kill; he couldn't pass the pile of reeking bodies, their organs spilling out on to the floor in a steaming, slimy, gut-turning mess. He retched as he realised that the blood on his hands had come from them.

Those bodies . . . he remembered that only this morning they had been living, moving, smiling beings. They had looked fierce and proud when they had galloped up the drive, the glint of the sun making jewels in the boy's eyes as he watched. Now their faces looked empty, and their fine, embroidered clothes were torn and bloodied; their long, curled hair had fallen dead around their shoulders.

He recalled that he had been sitting in his favourite spot that morning, in the windowsill of the library, looking down into the courtyard below. The five horses of the deputation – all of them grey, except one roan – had trotted into the courtyard, their hooves clattering on the old stone. Sam and Tim, the ragged, stick-thin kitchen boys, had run out to meet them and tether the horses; they gave them water, but they did not bring them food – they had eaten the last of the oats themselves that morning.

Then he had thought he knew why the deputation had come. He had heard gossip in the kitchens, that the King was going to take his father's Manor away. When the ruffians who lurked around Oldstone Manor had heard the news they had all either run off or sunk into drunken stupors. He'd passed one on the stairs, filthy and stinking in his own vomit.

His father had strode into the library, grabbed him and hefted him downstairs to Great Hall. There the men had been waiting, standing in a line, their clothes clean and their faces smiling. They had spoken kind words to him. He hadn't answered, because his father had told him not to speak.

One of them, younger than the rest, with laughing eyes and a blue tunic, and long brown hair, the one who had ridden on the roan, had thrown him an apple; as the young man caught his gaze, his eyes stopped laughing.

The boy gobbled up the apple, peel, pips and all. It was the first thing he had had to eat, apart from crusts, for almost two days. He had enjoyed feeling the sweet acid seep into his stomach.

He had been going hungry since his mother died.

Now, as his father stood, the memory of his mother came to him: the last time he had seen her was when she had been hanged, dressed in the white shift which she wore in bed. They hadn't even allowed her to dress properly.

He remembered how sick he'd felt, and how ashamed, as he had run away into the woods, aiming for one of the watchtowers where he often hid, but his father's men had caught him and brought him to the front of the house. The stink of a blackened hand over his mouth came back to him, and he retched at the thought of it. He tried to think of something else, and came back to his mother . . .

His mother's face, still calm and beautiful, and those hands that he had swung on so many times, the little dip in her nose, the mole above her right cheekbone. But he could not stop himself from reliving the moment when the stool beneath her had been kicked away, and how he had caught the dolour in her eyes.

She had looked right at him, he had seen her lips move, and he had known that she was saying, 'I love you . . .' But sometimes at night he saw her face, pale and anguished, and instead she was saying, 'Save me . . .' He had done nothing to save her.

After that, he remembered, his life had changed. The boy had heard his father being called a wizard, a necromancer. His father was reaching out to others, the boy had discovered; there were rumours of conspiracy, of revolution, of a league of nightmare and shadow. He had been thrown out of his comfortable rooms, and put in a tiny attic bedroom, where his bed was a small pallet of dirty straw, and the cobwebs that garlanded the beams were the only decorations. Where before he had played with pages and squires, he had been left with only his nurse, Jemima.

As he watched her now, shrieking and babbling, he recalled how she would clutch him to her apron, muttering about dark times. Half of the things she said he didn't understand. She wittered about blood lines, and destinies.

The boy had watched his father gamble and drink all day and all night, in the smoke of the Hall, surrounded by cut-throats, thieves, magicians and murderers. Wagons full of bottles came up the drive to the Manor; endless beer barrels came up the river; but the crops failed and the apples rotted. Villainous-looking people came from all around to see the boy's father; he was endlessly closeted with them, his plottings kept so secret that even those who whispered a word were slaughtered.

It was too much for the boy. He had seen his father degenerate from a kind man into a monster. And now his father was a cold-blooded murderer, who had killed the people who had given him an apple. He wasn't going to stand for it. The memory of his mother overflowed inside him. He stopped shaking and, without really knowing why, ran out into the middle of the room.

'Sir . . .'

His father looked at him with hell-fire in his eyes. 'Pray now, what is it, sirrah – thou beetle-headed whelp?' he said, spitting blood. One of his teeth had come loose, and he expelled it with relish.

The boy felt anger and hatred welling up in him. 'You killed my mother. You told them to hang her. She didn't do anything. She was my mother. And now you killed these people. They were kind . . .' The boy ran at his father and beat him with his fists. His father stopped him easily with one arm.

'Oh ho, my little warrior, and what are you going to do about it?' His father raised up his sword and held it against the boy's throat. 'What wilt thou do, thou whelp, thou abortive *hedgepig*?' The boy gulped at the familiar *thou*, feeling the cold, toothy steel against his skin.

'My Lord! Don't touch the boy!' whimpered

13

Jemima. 'He's only a little one! He's my little one . . .' Her red-rimmed eyes peered out from under her great frilly cap, and they were filled with tears. She rushed at his father, flailing at him with her tiny, bird-like arms.

'God's blood, will you be silent!' shouted his father, and thrust her aside. The boy watched, aghast, as a stream of blackness crackled out of his hand into Jemima, and she screamed and fell dead on to the pile of bodies. He turned to his son, snarling, ''Sdeath! . . . I should get rid of you too, hag-seed, spawn of your filthy, crazy witch-mother that you are. I should send you back into the sweat and brimstone whence you crawled . . .' He raised his sword and aimed at the boy's throat. 'Goodbye, my little one, my sweet gentleman.' The boy tensed, tears dampening his reddened cheeks.

'Father . . .' He felt the swish of the sword as it swung back. Then he heard a creak, and a rush, and a terrible thundering. The huge doors to the Hall banged open.

A strong, foreign voice called out, 'Wentlake de la Zouche, by order of the Blood, put down that sword!'

Wentlake turned round slowly. Two men had entered the room. They were heavily armed and wore clothing strange to the boy – blue, shimmering tunics, and long cloaks that skimmed the floor. They were tall, slender, but looked strong, and alike – a long face, clean-shaven, brown hair that fell in short waves. They had muskets and other weapons the boy did not recognise, that shone and hummed. Wentlake guffawed.

'So the reinforcements have arrived, have they? Do you think that you can hurt *me*?' He made a dismissive gesture with his hands. 'Give me leave to finish my business.' He turned back to the boy.

Then there was a shot. One of the men had fired a musket. His father staggered, but did not fall. It was enough for him to turn his attention away from his son. The boy fled behind an oak table that stretched down one side of the Hall. Blanche and Fairfax ran to him, and he felt fleeting comfort from them. He clung to one of the table legs, feeling the shapes of vines and leaves underneath his fingers.

'The Book, my Lord,' said one of the men. 'Show us where the Book is!'

'The power of the Book is mine. None can stand against it.'

'We are more powerful than you think,' said the first man. 'And we have orders from one stronger than you.'

Wentlake snorted. 'You mean the dead old man? The one that was plaguily tricked by a *woman*? Rubbish!' he spat.

'You may be the Scion of the Blood, but for you true knowledge is impossible.'

'It is what I have been seeking all my life. I *will* attain it. I have understood the Book more than any other who came before me. They were all fools, maggoty, deluded fools.' Derision spilled from every syllable.

The first man spoke, his face set and his voice low. 'You have corrupted the Book. You have broken the tenets of your Guardianship. You are apostate, heretic, traitor. We are Harbingers of the Old One. Though he wakes not, his mind is still quick. And this is the message we bring.'

And then the room was filled with a deep-red light, and to the boy it felt like the most comfortable thing that he had ever felt, like when he'd been with his mother and father, when he was younger, and his father had given him branches of apple blossom and his mother had laughed. Then he sensed something painful around the edges – things that, when he looked at them too closely, began to make him feel dizzy and confused, as if he were falling out of Great Hall into another world.

He could hear his father laughing loud and long. He mustered up enough courage to peer over the table again and saw that one of the men had fallen, his musket clanging to the floor. And then the light became stronger, and warmer, and his father stopped laughing, and started screaming, and it was a scream that tore the boy's heart from his chest, and he cried out and the screaming got louder and louder and the light got hotter and hotter and the boy was torn between hatred and love until something in the room snapped and it stopped.

'Soft, little one . . . you can come out now . . .' said a voice. A gentle voice.

He looked over the table cautiously. When nothing happened he stood up, slowly. One of the men was beckoning to him. There was no sign of his father. Where he had been standing, in the centre of the Hall, there was now a black book, squatting and steaming like a devilish toad.

And yet it was also beautiful. The boy felt a connection with it. Without knowing what he was doing, he ran to it. It was the most exquisite thing he had ever seen – crafted out of what looked like black leather, with nothing else to embellish it. The blackness of it . . . as he stared at it he felt something he had never felt before except in dreams, that he was falling into a great space and that something was approaching him . . . Voices brought him back to the Hall.

'My Lord,' said the two men, and knelt to him.

'Why are you kneeling to me? Where is my father?'

said the boy, and his mind felt as empty as the vast spaces he knew existed between the planets.

'He is only small,' said one of the men. The one who had spoken moved forward, and took him gently by the shoulder. 'Your father is dead,' he said, and the boy felt a sad sickness in his stomach. At the same moment Blanche and Fairfax came running out and leapt on to him, licking away his tears. He pushed them down, gratefully.

'Do you know of the birthright of your family?' said the man.

The boy shook his head.

'Your father has corrupted it. He has sown a seed of evil. It will take four centuries to leach out, and by that time there will be another who will seek to corrupt the line again. You have no choice.'

'What must I do?'

'You must undo the work your father started. You will live your life in this Manor, but you will always be fighting against the Other World, and when you pass from this world you will continue the fight. He has poisoned the Book. You cannot use it.'

The boy felt repulsed. This book was the cause of all the evil in the Manor. 'I do not want it. Destroy it,' he said.

'But that cannot be done, my Lord. It holds secrets

old and great, and you are bound to it by your very blood.'

'Then hide it from me. Bury it,' he said, revolted that something so hideous could be a part of him.

'So it will be done. Because of your father, you will be the sole bulwark against the Other World for generations to come, as many as there are leaves on the trees, until the day when the Book is found, and restored to the glory of the past and to its rightful heir. Your ancestors, mighty warriors, held this Manor for the King, and upheld all that is good and noble and true. Knowledge and art grew strong here, and the flame of concord was kept when all around the darkness howled. Here was the seed of civilisation sown, and here will be the end.'

All the boy could think of was the gloating, heavy-lidded look in his father's face; he was conscious of the lure of the Other Book as it was held in front of him, and he could feel it encroaching upon him. He shrank into himself. He could not imagine how it could be the source of good.

'Is there no other way?' said the boy.

'None,' said the man.

They marched out to the pond, where there stood a tall oak tree, and the two men dug with spades, and the boy dug too, with his hands, scrabbling and scraping, and when he was too tired and his hands were bloody and caked in mud, he sat and watched them dig, until they had dug deep enough for the thing to be buried, far from his mind.

It took two hours by the church clock. Only Blanche and Fairfax stayed close by, faithful as ever, lifting their voices in support.

When the peals of the bell rang out six times into the leaden air, one of the men pulled the boy close.

'It must be sealed,' he said and, without warning, he stabbed his dagger into the boy's side. Ignoring his half-screams, half-wheezes, the man held the dagger over the book, and blood fell on to it. The men put the last of the earth back and patted it down with spades. The boy felt his side. It was just a shallow cut, though it hurt deeply.

'You have a hard task ahead of you,' said the man. 'Do it well and your line will be restored. One will come, centuries ahead, who will aid you in restoring the Book. We can do no more.'

Through his gasps, the boy squeezed out a question. The man answered curtly. 'As it was cut off, so it will be restored.'

A haze of light surrounded the men as they disappeared, leaving the boy on his own by the pond, holding his side as the blood seeped out of him,

Blanche and Fairfax licking his hands. He sat there in the rain and wept.

The boy grew up, and married a sweet, button-nosed young gentlewoman from a neighbouring Manor. He kept himself from Society; always he fought terrible battles against the darkness that threatened the world. He could never enjoy the rays of the sun, for they fell fractured around him, like a shapely glass vase that falls broken to the floor.

Nothing ever grew on the ground above where the poisoned book lay. The spot was marked with a pillar, and only the boy knew what was under it.

He, who had been called whelp, and hag-seed, and had seen the destruction of both his parents, had his own children, who knew nothing of the horrors their father had faced, but only guessed at it in the depths of his scarred eyes. He loved them fully, but distantly, and they grew apart from him. They had their own children, and there came a time, when the cellars were full, when light streamed through the clean windows of Great Hall, when there was a Hanoverian on the throne and the world was changing, that the old man left this world, and passed into the Other World, there to fight every day to pay for his father's sin, always watching for the one who would bring him peace.

Secrets were lost, and things were hidden, curses were laid and seeds were sown. Things crept across the boundaries that should not have crept across, and sat in the darkness and waited.

Two

omething was charging at Edward, hurtling through the mist that was as thick as treacle around him, and he couldn't get out of its way. He thrashed, and woke up gasping, the sick taste of fear still sticking in his mouth, his brain twanging like a trapped nerve. A blurry object juddered into his vision. For a moment he thought it was some demon that had hurtled out of his nightmare . . . but then it resolved itself into the ordinary face and body of Munro, who slept in the next bed to him. He was tugging at Edward's duvet.

It was a grim, sluggish day, a sense of foreboding hovering in the air like a vulture.

'Wake up, Pollock!' Munro was shouting. 'Ferrers has already been in. You're late!'

'What day is it?' Edward asked, the words gargling in his mouth. He blinked, two or three times, the

23

dream hot and foaming in his grasp. He still felt he was inside it. This was not unusual, for Edward dreamed a lot: intensely vivid dreams, where every detail was stark and clear, and he could smell and touch what was going on. His dreams were, to tell the truth, mostly about quite boring things like being late for lessons and winning tennis matches; but there were some which were tinged with something darker, where he felt as if he was exposed, and vulnerable, to something he could not define.

'It's the greatest day of them all!' said Munro, who somehow managed to be energetic even at seven in the morning. 'It's a wuh-whu-Wednesday! Come on, Pollock, get up!' He swung his towel around his head, hitting Edward with it, before scampering off in the direction of the bathroom – which was freezing cold, though summer approached.

Edward groaned, rolled over and went back to sleep, until Munro, Peake and the other boys in his dorm turned over his mattress. He got up woozily, put his mattress back on his bed and promptly fell asleep again.

It was Mrs Ferrers the matron who woke him up. 'How long have you been at Oldstone, Edward?'

'What?' he said, muffled by the duvet he'd put over his head.

'I *said*, how long have you been at Oldstone?'

Edward pushed back his duvet grumpily.

'Since I was five. Seven years.'

'So you're as well aware as I am that breakfast is at eight o'clock!'

'Yes, Mrs Ferrers.'

'So I'd get up if I were you.' Mrs Ferrers was inclined to be nice to Edward. She remembered him on his first day, as a small, rowdy, gangly boy. Over the years this rowdiness had been distilled into a gentle, faintly rebellious melancholy.

'Come on, Pollock. Milo's getting cross.' Milo was Edward's hippo. When Edward had first arrived at the Manor, his jacket was about eight sizes too big for him and he still slept with Milo. Milo now sat on Edward's chair on top of a teetering pile of books.

'Milo can't get cross,' said Edward, though he secretly half-believed that he could, which was why he kept him on his chair. 'That's a ridiculous thing to say.' He patted Milo on the head.

'Come on, then,' said Mrs Ferrers, smoothing down the pleats of her dark blue skirt. She always wore a string of pearls, whatever she was wearing; she fiddled with it now, impatiently.

With a groan like a sea monster Edward pulled himself up and out of bed, putting his bare feet on to the floor. It was comfortably, solidly real. He always felt that he stood on the edges of things, that he had some deeper access to what was unseen; to feel the bare carpet beneath his feet reminded him that there was a normal world, and he was in it.

'Good,' said Mrs Ferrers, and rustled out of the dorm.

Edward flicked back his blond hair, which was always far too long for his headmaster's liking. He didn't like Wednesdays. He dressed, pulling on shorts that were getting too tight for him, struggled into his house shirt, and went gropily down the back stairs to Kakophagy. When he'd first come to the school, he hadn't known what Kakophagy meant, and no one had explained it to him. He'd worked out, eventually, that it was Greek, and meant 'bad eating place', which the boys called the dining hall as a joke.

After breakfast – which was a mess of sausages, black pudding, tomatoes and toast – everybody trailed out round the Manor to line up for assembly in Great Hall. Pushing, shoving, arguing and fighting, the boys were silenced by a look from the headmaster, and, subdued, traipsed in. Today, it being a Wednesday, assembly was given by Mr Flayton, the dullest teacher imaginable.

Edward plonked himself down on a bench after

prayers next to his first cousin and best friend, Will Strangore, who looked like a large, cross owl. Flayton began, without any preamble or joke, to talk about the Manor House, which had already been there when the Normans came. He was telling a story about one of William the Conqueror's knights, who had been so enchanted by the gorgeous lady who lived there that he laid down his sword and married her on the spot.

'That sucks,' whispered Edward to Will. It sounded to him like Susan in the Narnia books giving up battles and adventure for lipstick and invitations. He spent the rest of assembly staring glassily at the portraits that hung around Great Hall. There were two in particular that caught his attention today – a large one of a fierce-looking cavalier that hung above the great mantlepiece, and a smaller one of a rather sad-looking gentleman that was almost hidden under the beams. He knew which one he preferred.

Will was covertly reading a science book.

'You're such a geek, Strangore,' said Edward in an unguarded moment, earning him a dirty look from O'Brien the science teacher. As if assembly wasn't bad enough, Eudoky (which was the reason, Edward had found out, that the dining room was called 'Kakophagy' – it meant in Greek 'good teaching place') had double science that morning. They grabbed their books from their form room, and went up to the lab.

The laboratory was a smelly, tatty building that had been built as a temporary measure thirty years before. But as usual there wasn't enough money for a new one, though the paint was peeling off and sometimes in winter rain came through the roof and they put a bucket underneath the leak and pretended it wasn't there.

Mr O'Brien was crazy and slightly suspect. He wore very bright jumpers and had very short, cropped hair which he never allowed to grow any longer.

The two cousins were sitting at the back of the class. Will as usual had got everything right, and Edward was dreamily copying down the results without really thinking about them.

O'Brien's dog was snuffling around Edward's feet. The dog was called Imp, short for Imperative, the boys were told, but Edward thought it really was a sort of devil. 'Imperative' was one of Mr O'Brien's favourite words. He was saying it now.

'It is imperative, boys, that you do not put too much acid in!'

'That scabby dog!' muttered Edward. 'Why does O'Brien let him into lessons?'

He shifted his feet to get rid of the small, yappy instrument of terror which was sniffing round his shoes. It had no effect, except to make Imp growl a little.

'Don't move!' said Will. 'Don't forget what happened to Earnshawe.'

'What happened to Earnshawe?' asked Edward through gritted teeth, holding himself very still.

'Imp ate him! Whole. And left nothing but his fingernails. And some toffees which were in his pocket.'

'Don't blame him, if they were school toffees!' They are *rank*.' Edward made a gagging movement with his fingers. Imp let out a whimper.

'Quiet!' said O'Brien. 'Or you're out – with a double kappa!'

(A kappa was a bad mark – short for 'kakistos', which meant 'the worst' in Greek. The opposite was 'aristos', for 'the best'. The boys called them 'kaks' and 'nobles' for short; 'nobs' for even shorter – especially if someone like Strangore got too many of them. Only the teachers called them kappas and alphas.)

Imp scudded off at the sound of O'Brien's voice, back to the feet of his adored master.

'Wouldn't be such a bad punishment,' Edward whispered to Will, and raised a small smile on his cousin's owlish face. O'Brien's face darkened, and he began to say something admonitory, but luckily at that moment, Montgomery, who was the bell boy, ran out to signal the end of lessons, and the boys made their slow way down to lunch, dropping their books off at Eudoky on the way.

Edward and Will piled into Kakophagy with all the other boys. The dark, red-painted walls made Edward feel at home – warm and comfortable. Whilst everyone else clattered in noisily, he hovered for an almost unnoticeable moment on the threshold, and filled his lungs with the permanent stale smell of sausages, hot-pots and roast potatoes. The ornately framed portraits of ancient headmasters dead and gone, and boards with the names of old head boys and people who'd won scholarships painted proudly in gold made him feel part of something bigger than himself. One day he hoped to see his name on that board, although he would never admit that, even to Will.

The two boys took their places behind the benches at one of the twenty wooden tables that stood in severe rows. There was a sudden silence as the headmaster, Mr Fraser, said grace in Latin, and then everyone sat down.

Why does O'Brien have to be head of our table, on top of everything else? thought Edward as he pulled out the bench. He looked gloomily at the lasagne which was piled up crustily in a vast vat in front of O'Brien. It looked like it had been scraped out of a prison's dustbins and dumped back on to the plates, barely warmed up. There were no rats at Oldstone Manor, thought Edward, probably because they were being used for the lasagne. Squirrels too should keep a wide berth of the kitchen.

O'Brien, without even asking, piled up the most enormous heap of steaming, stinking lasagne, before handing it down the table to Edward. He kept his eye on Edward all lunchtime so that he had no chance to scrap it in one of the bowls that stood on the table for that purpose. As Edward was forcing a second, revolting forkful into his mouth, he noticed Mandy out of the corner of his eye. She was the daughter of one of the kitchen staff and went to school in the village. She often came to the Manor at lunchtime to help out her mother, and now she was taking some plates out. She turned round to pick up another and caught his eye, and Edward made a face at her, inadvertently swallowing a huge piece of lasagne that he had been holding in his mouth for quite some time, in the hope that he would be able to spit it out into the scrapping bowl. No such luck, he thought, as he watched Mandy stifle a laugh and head back quickly into the kitchen.

Further down the table, Edward saw the school bully Guy Lane Glover tormenting his cousin Will – punching him under the table, knocking his cutlery off and drinking his water. Will of course would never say anything, which seemed to make Guy torment him more.

But the brightly-sweatered O'Brien continued to

watch Edward. He believed that if the boy were given enough football and enough science (and enough lasagne), he would somehow magically come to like them. Aversion therapy, or something like that. All of which meant that on this particular Wednesday Edward had to settle to being linesman at the football match.

Every Wednesday and Saturday there was a match against another school. Rugby and cricket Edward could cope with. Tennis, basketball, hockey – he could even do cross-country running. But football . . . it seemed to him like an advanced form of torture.

So on this Wednesday, an hour or so after lunch, Edward was reluctantly standing behind the goal, a flag hanging limply in his hand. The large pitches stretched out either side of him. Parents huddled together at one end. In the distance some boys were playing cricket in the nets. Behind him was another field. Third-form boys straggled beside him.

Even though it was May, and the beginning of the Trinity term, there had been a grudge match against their local rivals which had been postponed and post-poned until now. There was much honour at stake, and both schools took it seriously. O'Brien was totally caught up in the game, so Edward handed the flag to one of the third formers and began to sidle away. He was standing as far back from the pitch as he could. The shouts and drama of the game already felt distant and unreal. The light, warm drizzle of the late May afternoon was pleasantly dampening his skin.

The morning's dream was returning to him. He'd had it before. But the dream had always changed to winning the tennis tournament (not likely), or driving a Ferrari (even less likely). This morning it hadn't. This time it had been so vivid, so frighteningly solid, that Edward had been trembling all day. Something was breaking through the delicate membrane which, unknown to him, surrounded his world.

He was now about twenty feet from the line. There was a field behind him, bounded by a stone wall. He thought he could sneak into it, just for a few minutes, and sample the cool wetness of the grass. He could lie on the ground, listening to the complete and eerie silence, make stories out of the shapes of trees against the skies, and try to unravel the mistiness of the nightmare that haunted him.

Turning his back on the field, Edward looked at the football match. O'Brien wasn't likely to notice that he'd gone. Oldstone was winning, and O'Brien was too caught up in the game to notice that Edward Pollock, a lowly linesman, had skived off. The ball wouldn't come his way, anyway. He was behind the home goal end, and all the action was up against the opposition's.

A scuffle was developing on the pitch between Guy Lane Glover and one of the Southey boys. O'Brien had dived in to stop it, and was giving Lane Glover a good ticking off and threatening him with a yellow card. The noses of the oil-skin wearing parents were all turned to the other end of the pitch. Edward could move away, and get some peace. He chose his moment to escape carefully, and melted quietly, like a shadow into the greater darkness, and disappeared through the gap in the stone wall.

Edward rested against the wall, just on the inside of the field. He felt as if he had slipped into a different world. Light slanted through the clouds, falling through stirring, rustling trees. Tiny splashes of rain made everything look fresh and clean. The sky here seemed to be a different colour, deeper and richer.

The tracings of the trees against the sky were like etchings. He stared around the field, taking in the graceful movement of every blade of grass. A gentle breeze was rustling his damp hair. He slumped down, and curled into the stones, closing his eyes. He was beginning to feel listless, as if he were underwater. Everything was far away, and the dull, dark-red tinge of the sky seeped through his eyelids. The breeze sounded like the distant breaking of waves on a fabled shore. All the enforced rituals of school – the match, the labs, the lasagne – were disappearing, turning into tiny specks of annoyance in the far distance. Everything was calm. He had managed to disperse all thought of the nightmare. He didn't want to analyse it, to understand it. He wanted to erase it. But just as he thought he had, it came back to him . . . and then he heard something.

A gentle, ripping noise coming from a far corner of the field, nearest to the church. He could hear a faint whimpering, too. He cautiously opened his eyes. Through the drizzle he could distinguish something moving, a dark shape, bobbing up and down, in a way that made Edward feel disgusted.

A force he did not understand drew him towards it. He reared up from the wall and began to run. The whimpering had an excited edge to it. He came nearer, and the shape resolved itself into the horrific terrier, Imp. He was snuffling, and tormenting something black. Edward ran up to the dog, shouting as loud as he could. It turned jealously, and growled.

'Imp! Get away! Get away!' he shouted. Imp growled again, baring his teeth, saliva dripping from his maw. His hackles were up and he shivered with anger.

'Go on! Get away!' shouted Edward, waving his

arms at the beast, trying to make himself bigger than he was, dredging up some half-forgotten hint from a book read years ago. He wasn't sure that it was working because Imp seemed ready to spring, coiled up like a deadly viper. He didn't dare stop yelling and run away. He was afraid that the dog would leap after him and be on him, in a second. And no way did he want to come into contact with those stinking teeth, and end up like Earnshawe – eaten alive. Imp's eyes, like those of an assassin, glared at the boy, gleaming, as if he knew something Edward didn't.

Edward was just mustering enough courage to make a rush at Imp when the dog acted as if he had heard a whistle or a command that Edward could not detect. Imp's ears flattened, his eyeballs looked as if they were going to jump out of his skull, and he made a strange gulping sound and ran from the field. Edward shuddered from the cold and from adrenalin.

He looked down at the ground.

It was a raven. It was massive, almost as big as Imp. No doubt he hadn't attacked it out of hunger. O'Brien fed him to the brim with chicken and salmon. The creature had ravaged it out of pure spite. The bird was mangled enough to cause a deep tug in Edward's gut, which became a ball of tight emotion in his throat. He knelt on the ground, in the wet coolness of the long grass.

He didn't then know that it was odd for a raven to be there, in the south-east of England. He didn't think that someone could have sent it there, for reasons he couldn't know. He didn't then know that sad eyes were watching him from another world; that someone had fixed their notice upon him.

The bird was enchanting and it had been alive. Now it had been destroyed by something brutal and unnecessary. Edward hoped that it hadn't been alive for long after Imp had got hold of it. Its eyes were dull. He could not tell if they had seen him. He didn't know if there was any truth in the story that the last thing a creature sees before death is imprinted on its eyeballs, but he was disturbed to see his own reflection staring back at him.

He picked up the raven. The feathers were almost pleasant to touch. A fly had settled on a scrawny part of its neck. He brushed it away, but it returned. He looked around for somewhere to put the corpse, and remembered that the field he was in was next to the church. He ran towards the other side, away from the pitches, his football socks coming down, the grass whipping his bare legs, and clambered over the wall, jumping down awkwardly into a muddy flowerbed. It was raining harder now and his shirt was clinging to his skin.

He felt himself drawn to the biggest monument in the churchyard, a stone block, taller than he was, with carvings around the edges of leaves and vines that looked like intertwined Ms and Vs. He ran his fingers over a large shield, feeling the bumps and grooves of its design. It had an inscription under it, in Latin, but he couldn't read it because it was too faint. The crest was a bird, poised for flight. There was a name on the tomb, almost rubbed away. He could just about make it out:

TRISTRAM DE LA ZOUCHE

A curious name, gentle and fierce at the same time.

He hoisted himself up on to the monument, keeping the bird in the crook of his arm, and scrabbled for the centre. He laid the raven down on its back, with its wings outstretched. He studied it, and the thought came into his mind that it was an angel, lost and fallen. More flies came to it and he tried to bat them away, but they kept returning. And still he felt that he had something more to do. His haunches were beginning to hurt. He needed something to dignify the raven, to make its death worthwhile. He leapt down from the monument, and decided that he would pick some flowers. He took them from the beds, and from other graves, choosing not white lilies but bright red, yellow and pink blooms. When he had his arms full he climbed back up on to the monument, scuffing his knee, and laid them around the raven. He sat back on his heels to look at it, filled with serenity.

Afterwards, Edward couldn't say how long he had been there. Time seemed to be a little different.

The vicar, Reverend Smallwood, a tall and expansive man, found him there, sitting on top of the monument, gazing at the raven. He tapped him gently on his wet shoulder.

'Good evening, Pollock,' he said, with a friendly gesture. 'Are you all right?'

Edward didn't answer. He didn't know what to say. He felt more than a little foolish.

'Well, my boy. Is there anything that you'd like to tell me?' the Reverend said, peering down.

Edward couldn't cover up the dead bird, and shook his head. He got down, jarring his body as he came into contact with the ground.

'The poor thing would have died one way or another, you know,' said the Reverend.

Edward looked at him. Smallwood hadn't understood. It wasn't the death so much. It was that the raven's story had been brutally cut off. There was a difference. It didn't seem right.

'All the same,' the Reverend continued, 'there was no need to pluck up all these flowers, now, was there?' His jolly tones grated on Edward's ear.

Edward shook his head slowly. He hadn't really thought about it. He didn't know what he had been thinking. He could see Smallwood looking at him searchingly – at his muddied knees and hands, and the rain dripping down his face.

'I think,' the Reverend said, stretching his arms behind his back casually, 'that you and I should take a walk back to the school, and that we should see Mr Fraser. Do you think that would be a good idea?' He always spoke as if he were in public – perhaps because he had once been a barrister. Edward always wondered why he'd given up his wig for a dustier cassock.

The odd pair walked through the churchyard. The Reverend was a little ahead of Edward. The rain had let off, and the clouds were clearing quickly, as if they had been ripped apart. The graveyard was quiet. Smallwood talked as they went. Edward drank in the words, but did not really taste them, letting them flow over him. They wandered slowly past the entrance to the church. It was dark, and sombre, and nothing stirred inside. Birds perched on some of the headstones of the graves, and in his mind Edward made them mourners for the raven.

Soon Smallwood and Edward came to the gate that opened into the courtyard of Oldstone Manor, just below Edward's dormitory window. The gate was wrought iron, rusty and ancient. It was topped with spikes, as if it had been designed to keep something out. As they passed through it, Edward felt that he was returning to what was solid and real again, and his mind became clearer. He ran over what had happened and could not understand what he had done. It was the sort of thing that he would have done when he was much younger, and he and his brothers and sisters would bury dead baby birds in cotton wool in shoeboxes.

As they came through the mellow stone of the courtyard, the church clock struck six. I've missed the end of the match, thought Edward, so at least some good has come out of it. He'd also missed five o'clock roll call. Everyone is going up to do their prep now, he thought.

The headmaster's study gave on to the courtyard, and had the same view over the valley as Edward's dorm. Smallwood knocked on the door, which was open, letting in the cool air, and went in. Edward crept in behind him, not sure whether he was about to be punished or absolved.

He saw Mr Fraser sitting at his creaky red-leather-topped desk. It was covered in messy piles of papers, and a computer hummed irritably on one corner. A half-smoked cigarette lay in a stone ashtray by his hand. Fraser stubbed it out as they entered and picked up a clutch of papers almost defensively, before he yawned, covering his mouth with the sheaf. He was peering inquisitively at the computer, as if he was only half aware of what it was doing.

'Damned mysterious, these things. Ah, the Rev. Good evening.'

'Good evening, Headmaster.' The Reverend was almost courtly, giving a little bow that no doubt he had used to charm judges in court.

'And hello, Pollock,' Fraser said, as if he had just noticed him, giving Edward a wink that creased up one side of his face, revealing his yellow teeth.

'Evening, sir,' he said, half-heartedly.

'What can I do for you?' said the headmaster. He sounded very much as if he had other things to worry about.

'I just brought Pollock in to see you. I found him in the churchyard. He's a little distracted. *Distrait*, if you will,' said the Reverend, and laughed fruitily.

'Thank you, Rev.'

'Now if you'll excuse me, I must get back for Vespers.' The Reverend smiled at Edward, and patted him on the back. As Smallwood was leaving, Edward saw him exchange a glance with the headmaster before striding out of the study, back across the courtyard into his own domain.

Fraser waited till he had gone. Then he swung around in his battered swivel chair, and faced Edward fully. His black, curlyish hair was tousled and his leathery skin was creased. He laid down the papers which he had been clutching, and smoothed them repeatedly. The computer beeped. He jumped slightly at the noise, and clicked his tongue.

'What on earth does that beep mean? I haven't told it to do anything . . . Oh, do sit down, old chap,' he said. Edward sat down in the chair in front of the desk. 'So you've missed roll call, have you?'

Edward nodded.

'And skiving off games, too. We've had this before, haven't we?'

He nodded, again.

'What are we going to do with you?'

Edward remained silent.

'Can you tell me why you were late? What were you doing in the churchyard?' said Fraser, a little more forcefully.

The trouble was that Edward couldn't tell him. It was all dreamlike now. If he didn't understand his own actions, how on earth could Fraser? For a moment Edward thought about confessing everything, and then

43

was prevented by the thought that Fraser would think he was a lunatic or worse. He murmured something.

'What was that, Pollock? Speak up.'

He looked him right in the eye.

'You know I hate football, sir.'

'I do, Pollock, yes.'

'Well, I was bored at the match, sir, and I went through the field into the churchyard and went exploring round it, sir, and then I lost track of the time, sir, and the Reverend found me and I didn't realise it was so late, sir.' He said all this very quickly.

Fraser looked at him. 'Is that the truth, Pollock?'

'Yes.'

Fraser smiled, and showed all of his yellow teeth, like little moons, pitted and cratered by many decades of bad eating.

'Well, Pollock. I know you don't like football. But it is very good for you – not just physically – and you must learn to do things that you do not like – even things that you hate. Ninety per cent of life, you'll find out soon enough, is rather dull. The other ten per cent makes it worthwhile.'

Only ten per cent, thought Edward. Not great.

Fraser looked at the clock on the wall. 'I think that you will be doing your prep in the library today, under my supervision.'

This wasn't such a bad punishment. Edward relaxed.

'Go on, then, off you go. Get changed first. Ten minutes.'

Supervised prep in the library was a standard punishment. But Edward loved the library. He loved its musty smells and ragged sofas. He would sit on the Victorian radiators in winter, when the boys still had to wear shorts and it was so cold their knees would go blue. 'Don't sit on the radiator, you'll get piles,' Mrs Ferrers used to say (although she never satisfactorily explained what piles were).

In the changing room, Edward stuck his head under a tap (to give the impression that he'd showered), hung up his games kit, pulled on his clothes and sprinted back to Eudoky, which nestled on its own near the tennis courts, a few hundred yards from a bend in the drive. Eudoky was empty, since everyone else was in the main teaching block. He opened up his desk, pulled out the books that he needed and ran out. He hesitated. He would have to take the long way round, which would make him late. The internal prefect in his mind was advising him against it, but he was compelled to go to the drive.

Boys were not allowed to go down the drive. Only prefects, masters and God (the headmaster used to joke) were allowed on it. Pausing just before he got there, he thought to himself that there could be absolutely no risk of anyone being on it at this point in the evening, so he ran down it, ignoring the little voice in his mind, his shoes clattering awkwardly.

And then, against all odds, he heard the sound of a car purring; it stopped, and he heard low voices.

Trying not to crunch the gravel, he reached a bend, and crouched behind a thick shrub, waiting to make a move. He was terrified of being caught by a master. He was panting more than he ought to have been. He tried to hold his breath, but it was difficult. He could not hear what the voices were saying, and strained his ears as much as he could. If he could identify which teacher it was, he'd know how lenient they might be. If it was O'Brien he'd have to go all the way back.

When he heard two women's voices, both very low, he relaxed a little. It was probably two of the matrons, back from their half-day out, who wouldn't mind so much. But as he prepared to leave the bush, he felt the hairs on the back of his neck prickle, as if a cold, invisible hand had just grazed it.

'Thank you, you may park up now,' said a cultivated voice; there was something rich and warm in it, but also something inhuman. Edward watched as the car slid off, and the women remained where they stood on the drive.

'Well, Mrs Phipps,' said the voice. 'I don't think we lost any time at all, do you?'

'You answered the call so quickly, my Lady,' said a rasping voice.

'You are right. Though how could you be anything other than right. It is useful to have . . . connections. And now, we are here. And I – I am *at home*.' She put great emphasis on those two words. *At home*. 'I think that I am very near my goal, Mrs Phipps. All my work, all those long, long years, and I think that we have nearly found it. It's such a shame that I lost . . .' Edward heard her pause, and then resume, resigned. 'Well, never mind. He knew what was coming to him, though.' She sounded sad for a moment, then sighed. Her voice took on a harder tone. 'Do you think that they'll resist?'

'We will break them, my Lady.' Edward shuddered. Mrs Phipps's voice was grating – an inversion of the other lady's.

'I suppose you could say that, although it *is* a little harsh. No, Phipps, we shall have to be very subtle. This place is full of obstinacy. But they won't be able to resist. Nobody will be able to resist.' She paused. 'They will be eating out of our hands. Once we have what we came for . . . and it is here, isn't it?'

'It's here, my Lady,' said the other. 'I know it is here.'

47

'I can *feel* it is here, Phipps, in my blood . . . it is part of me, remember . . .'

Edward's nerves were screaming at him to run. His reasoning held him back. He had to know more. He leant in closer. Only a slender branch separated him from the voices. He wondered if he could risk taking a look.

'All the signs have been pointing this way for years. We just needed that one, conclusive proof, and then it came. It is time to reclaim it.' She sounded proud and strong.

'And me, my Lady? You will not forget me? You who have *made* me.'

'Of course not.' But something in what she said made Edward feel she was not telling the truth. 'The power to do what one wills, the power to make others do as you will . . . power over matter, over life, over . . . what was that? Look, here! You, boy!'

Edward froze. He had not been able to stifle a cough, and it had come sputtering out. The branch had been pulled back and the lady was staring straight at him. He felt as if a phantom were around his neck, strangling him, and he sprang out of the bush and started to run.

But it was too late. A hand had gripped his shoulder, and he was forced round, and was face to face with the two ladies.

'Well, Phipps, looks like we've caught one already,' said the lady with the sophisticated voice. She had a long face, that was delicately featured and carefully made up. Her brown-blonde hair had been artfully arranged to look as if she hadn't spent much time on it. She was dressed in a dark green suit jacket that fitted her slim body perfectly, and if she hadn't been so well dressed, perhaps she might not have looked so beautiful. Intelligence shone in her eyes.

The other woman didn't say anything. She was older, with a face full of wrinkles, straggly, black-grey hair, and her blank, cold eyes stared at nothing. A black, shapeless dress was billowing around her, much more than the slight wind should allow.

'What are you doing hiding there? What did you hear?' the lady asked sharply.

'I didn't hear anything,' said Edward, feeling the woman's fingers pressing into his shoulder. 'I'm going to see Mr Fraser. Please, I'm going to be late.'

'I'd just like to ask you a few questions first.' The tall, elegant lady leant in closer.

Edward felt thoughts rising unbidden – first of the boy he had dreamt of that morning in the dark smoke of Great Hall, and the terrifying man who had been his father; and suddenly the snarling image of Imp, and then the raven in the churchyard. He wrenched himself free of her grip, and started running wildly, blindly, back up the way he'd come, gravel spraying from his shoes, full pelt, all the way around Oldstone Manor, past Eudoky and the empty tennis courts, down the side passageway and through the back door, up the spiral staircase and into the library. He was gasping with fear.

'Mr Fraser . . .' he wheezed. 'Mr Fraser . . .'

The headmaster looked up from where he was seated in a leather armchair, surrounded by tottering piles of papers, some of which looked as old and creased as his face. 'Late, Pollock? I'm afraid I can't supervise you. Something has come up which needs my urgent attention. I'm sure you won't cause any trouble. Goodnight.' He stamped down the stairs. Edward ran to the window and looked out at the drive.

The two ladies he had seen were entering the Manor. The younger one bore a look of intense fury; and as she came into Oldstone Edward thought that he saw her shudder – with fear, or excitement, he could not tell. Mrs Phipps flapped in after her, and to Edward she seemed insubstantial, a creature made from the night-mare he'd had that morning.

Three

dward watched the two women disappear inside. Then he moved away from the window and ran to the other side of the library, and curled up on the sofa, like a hedgehog. They had threatened him, in some obscure way, and he was on edge. Danger signals flashed through his body.

Here, in the corner of the vast library, he felt exposed. All these books could do nothing for him. Galahad could not leap out of *Idylls of the King* – he'd be too busy looking for the Grail anyway. Edward had no horn to blow, like in *Prince Caspian*, or a helpful Phoenix or Psammead. His thoughts rushed helter-skelter. He wondered if the ladies would recognise him if they saw him again. It occurred to him that they might not have had enough time to see what he looked like in the half-light of a May evening.

He went over the strange things that he had heard. They were here to find something that would bring them power. What was it the younger women had said? She had answered a call – but who had made it? Somebody in the Manor was in contact with them. *Nobody will be able to resist*, she had said. Edward feared what they might do when they found what they were looking for, here, in these walls which were his home and his sanctuary . . . *the power to do what one wills, power over matter, over life* . . . The words seemed almost mad as he recounted them to himself. He could not possibly have heard her say such things . . . but however much he tried to persuade himself that he hadn't, he still came back to it, and the sound of the other woman's voice as she had said *break* . . .

He imagined the two ladies storming up the stairs, terrible, furious, looking for the boy who had over-heard them. He wondered if his face would give it all away, and if he would crack under interrogation. He tried to remember all the techniques somebody had once told him to use in case he ever got caught by enemy spies, but could not conjure them up.

Five, then ten minutes passed. No one came up the stairs. Edward breathed out.

A kind of honey-light filled the room. The whole sky was like a glowing sword taken out of a forge fire before it cools. He turned on the sofa and gazed out of the window. Below him was the courtyard that he could also see from his bedroom window. The Manor filled three sides of it, and it was open to the valley, the church and the river on the fourth.

There was a pillar in the middle of the courtyard. It was a small stone construction with a flat top – there had probably been a sundial on it once. As he watched, it began to tremble, shaken by some unseen force, as if a minor earthquake were attacking it alone.

He looked around. Nothing else seemed to be moving. This was extraordinary, he thought. What was going on? The pillar shuddered, and then began slowly to topple over, tearing a great chunk of the courtyard with it, making a clunking, creaking noise, gathering momentum, until it hit the ground with a final, crashing racket. Edward covered his ears with his hands, the noise invading the calm of the library.

He was sure that for a second, just for the moment it takes a thought to leap from one synapse to another, he saw a figure bending over it, reaching into the earth and bringing something up; but then Mr Fraser ran out of his office, and the kitchen staff came running out too, and whatever imprint he had seen on the air had gone. He was alarmed. It seemed as if the earth had opened up for a purpose, as if something had been brought out for a reason. The thought that he had seen a ghost reclaiming a lost treasure flashed across his mind. He shivered, and he felt a pleasant edge of fear.

Frightened, he heard a movement behind him, scratching and swift, and spun round: again, faster than the shutter of a camera, he saw the figure reaching out towards the shelves and putting something down. And he saw it, unmistakeably, beckon to him. He blinked, and that was enough time for whatever it was to have gone. He felt a cold terror seize him.

He moved towards the shelves where the figure had stood just a moment ago. A ghost . . . a figment of his imagination, surely, he thought, fighting down the horror he felt rising in his mouth. His tongue was dry, and he swallowed, two or three times.

The shelves stretched all along the sides of the library, far up the walls, higher than Edward could reach. There was a moveable ladder, with three steps and a dark-red cushioned surface, that could be used to reach the very top shelves, which he would often swing on from side to side. He knew these books extremely well. Sometimes he would imagine that the library was the only place in the school – that everything else was destroyed, and that only the books would live on, whilst the cold, harsh winds blew dust through the empty halls.

Edward headed to the shelf where the figure had bent down, so briefly. He ran his finger along it and stopped at an unfamiliar texture – a calf-bound feel, like those in the antiquarian section.

He knelt down to have a look at the book. The title was printed in gold on the spine, and there was a small heraldic crest, some kind of bird, embossed on it. He bent his head sideways to read it. It was *Idylls of the King*. It was a series of poems by Alfred, Lord Tennyson, about the Knights of the Round Table. They had been studying it in English.

Edward read out the title of the book and the syllables felt like drops of wine on his lips. He took the book off the shelf. The noise of the boys below him, filing into supper, disturbed him for a moment. He glanced at the grandfather clock in the corner of the library. He felt no compulsion to join them, even though he was hungry. Their voices were a hazy backdrop to this object, which had suddenly become the focus of his being. He took it to his favourite part of the library – the corner seat, by the window, overlooking the valley and the courtyard below – and opened it up.

It was stamped with a familiar-looking coat of arms and dated in the late nineteenth century. The pages were delicate and light, and he began to turn them over gently.

A storm was coming, but the winds were still . . .

The unwelcome noise of clattering feet pulled him out of a trance. Somebody must have noticed that he was not in supper, and been sent to find him. He did not want to be parted from this book. It felt as if he had always been meant to find it, just as, in an odd way, it had felt that he had always been meant to find the savaged raven.

The door swung open. It was the worst person that it could have been. Guy Lane Glover swaggered in.

'What do you want, Glover?' said Edward, standing up and holding the book behind his back.

'Pollock, Pollock, weirdo Pollock!' said Glover. 'You're such a fre-eak.'

'You too, freako Glover. What do you want?'

'You've been busted, loser. O'Brien saw you weren't in supper. He told me to go and find you. He's really hacked off.'

'Well, now you've found me, so go away.'

Glover noticed the book Edward was trying to hide. 'And what's this? What's the little baby reading now?' He moved towards Edward, who clutched the book to his chest. 'Is it the little baby's diary?' Glover stopped in front of him and took on a theatrical pose. 'Oh, cruel, cruel world! It's all too much! Nobody likes me! Everybody hates me!' He looked at Edward, a dark slant on his face. 'Go on, Pollock, give me your diary!' Glover leapt at him, and grabbed the book. The two boys grappled for it, on the floor, and Edward fought with a ferocity that he had never shown before. He managed to wrench the book from Glover's grip and, just as he was about to get up and run, Glover punched him in the stomach. Edward threw the book away before he doubled up and brought Glover down with him. But out of the corner of his eye, Edward saw something fall out of it that looked like a piece of paper. He watched it float down and settle underneath the bookshelf. And something pulled at the inside of his gut, and drew him towards where that paper had fallen.

Then Glover punched him again, and Edward punched him back.

'Stop that! Stop it, at once!' It was Mr Fraser. He was standing in the doorway of the library, looking faintly bemused. Edward could hear mumblings behind the headmaster. 'Both of you, get to my office. Now!'

The two boys scrambled up.

'Go on. And Pollock, go and pick that book up and put it back where it belongs. Go on, now!'

Glover jumped up from the floor, catching Edward with the side of his foot, and then fled out, down the stairs and through the passageway to the office. Edward looked around and saw where *Idylls of the King* had landed by the shelves. He picked up his satchel and put it over his shoulder, and hesitated. He wanted to find the piece of paper. The green, gold spine of *Idylls* was glinting in the sunlight. As he picked it up he clumsily pretended to drop it, and knocked it under the shelf.

'Hurry up, Pollock! We haven't got all day.'

There was a tension in Fraser's voice which perplexed Edward. He could still hear low murmurings coming from behind the headmaster. He reached under the shelves for the book and his hand closed on something. He felt pierced by terror and a shockwave rippled up his arm. His mind filled with dark and fear.

He grabbed whatever it was and stuffed it into his satchel, his hand jerking back as if he had experienced a small electric shock, picked up *Idylls*, and scrabbled for the piece of paper he was sure had fallen out of it. He found it, and pulled that out too. He stuffed it into his pocket as he put *Idylls* back on the shelf, where he had found it.

'That book doesn't belong there, Pollock,' said Fraser.

'But sir, I found it there.'

'Well, it doesn't matter now, does it? Put it back

where it should be when I have finished with you. To my office, now. I am very disappointed, Pollock.' Edward watched as Fraser turned his leathery face to the people behind him. 'My apologies,' he said.

Edward's heart was beating very quickly. He walked past the headmaster and through the door. Standing behind Fraser, giving off an air of callous indifference, were the two ladies Edward had seen on the drive. Again, danger signals flashed throughout his body. He kept his head down and carried on walking. The ladies did not get out of his way.

The elegant lady seemed to be straining underneath the surface of her calm, like a hound that has scented its kill. As Edward edged past Mrs Phipps, she turned her head slowly to look at him, and her soft, flapping skin was pulled tightly across her face as she attempted to smile. Her eyes were like balls of fire burning into him. And then he ran as fast as he could, taking the stairs two at a time. He could still feel those eyes as he fled down the spiral stairs into the headmaster's office and closed the door behind him.

It was then that Edward noticed his bag was weighing down heavily upon his shoulder – which was strange, as there wasn't much in it. Surely whatever he had put in it couldn't be as heavy as that. It felt like a stone slab. He wriggled uneasily. Lane Glover was slouching in one of the easy chairs. He didn't look at Edward, but continued to stare glassily at the floor. Edward sat down in the hard chair by the desk.

Mr Fraser came in a few minutes later. He walked slowly behind his desk and glared at the boys. They both stood up when he entered. Guy left it slightly longer than Edward.

'Well, I would like to thank both of you,' said Fraser, sarcastically, 'for providing such an appropriate welcome for our important visitors.'

'Sorry, sir,' mumbled Edward. Guy said nothing.

'Do you know who that was?' Fraser said, searching Edward and Guy's faces. 'I don't suppose you do.'

'No, sir,' the boys said, in lilting unison; Edward realised it was probably the only time that he and Lane Glover had ever agreed on anything.

'*That* was one of the school's most generous bene-factors – without her family this school wouldn't even exist. That, you wonderful little boys, was Lady Anne de la Zouche.' Fraser announced her name with a certain amount of relish. The name chimed with something in Edward's memory – the name on the tomb he had just seen.

'Lady Anne is with her new . . . er . . . assistant, Mrs Phipps. Lady Anne is a school governor; and both are here on an extended visit to see what the school needs, and how best to . . . *improve* it. And for the moment, dear boys, it seems that what the school does not need, is you.' He paused for dramatic effect. 'Pollock!' he growled, and rapped his hand on the desk. 'Will you explain to me exactly why you were throwing school property around with such careless abandon?' He sneered, and his yellow teeth did not seem so friendly to Edward any more. 'May I remind you that this is not a centre for criminally delinquent children – although sometimes I may think it is. I expect this sort of thing from you, Lane Glover,' he said, sounding sad for a minute, 'but not from you, Pollock.' He clenched and unclenched his fingers. Edward could see he was fumbling for a cigarette in his trouser pocket.

Edward remained silent. The weight on his shoulder was getting heavier.

'No explanation, eh?' said Fraser. 'As usual. I am very disappointed in both of you.' He started to pace up and down. Edward longed to be able to get out. His shoulder was beginning to hurt.

'Lady Anne will have formed a very displeasing impression. Lady Anne is going to be the new Chairman of the Board of Governors,' he said, and he pronounced every syllable of her title with great emphasis. 'She has many . . . ideas.' Here he looked a little crestfallen, and the fire at least seemed to have

61

gone out of him. 'You have both earned the gracious honour of a double kappa.'

'That's not fair! I never threw anything!' said Glover plaintively. Edward willed him to shut up. He was only making it worse.

'I am sure that Pollock was not throwing books around because it pleased him, or because you asked him nicely, Glover. One more kappa for impertinence.' Mr Fraser was back to his old self now. Edward was relieved. 'Now you'd better go up to second prep.'

He seemed to have forgotten that Edward hadn't had any supper. Edward didn't mind at all. The weight in his satchel was what was interesting him. As he watched Fraser speak he could not help himself from feeling the bag surreptitiously. Something moved in it, and he jumped. Fraser looked back at him.

'Pollock, I can't supervise you in the library, and since you can't supervise yourself, you'd better go too. Quickly now.'

Edward stared as Lane Glover stormed out of the office, then he followed more slowly after him, out of the back entrance to Oldstone Manor and round the side. The two boys walked up to prep, Edward about ten feet behind Lane Glover.

Edward saw Glover hitting a stick against his shorts, taking a half-smoked cigarette out of his pocket which,

Edward thought, he must have nicked from Fraser's ashtray, and then swearing to himself and throwing the cigarette away.

'Stupid!' Edward heard him say, under his breath. He must have realised Edward was behind him, because he suddenly swung round and threw the stick at him.

Edward hurried to walk past him. His shoulder was aching again.

'I'm not going up,' said Glover. 'And you know something?'

'What, Glover?'

'Those two women. They're going to change things. They're going to shake this place up a bit.'

He's right, thought Edward. He sped on, as Lane Glover threw a stone that just missed him and hit a tree. They were going to change things. The weight on his shoulder shifted. As he turned the corner of the building, he ran straight into Mandy.

'Watch out!' she said, laughing.

'Sorry . . .' muttered Edward.

'What are you running from, anyway?'

'Oh . . . nothing . . .' said Edward, and then a thought occurred to him. 'Hey, Mandy, are you helping out your mother tonight?'

'Yeah, I am. Why?' she said.

'Well . . . it's just something I'm worried about. Two people came today . . . Lady Anne and Mrs Phipps. Lady Anne – she's in charge – she's tall, and *beautiful*. And Mrs Phipps . . . she's the total opposite. Can you . . . just keep an eye on them?'

'Sure,' said Mandy. 'What for?'

'It's a hunch.'

'You're mysterious, aren't you!' laughed Mandy. 'Well, I'll let you know if I see anything *strange . . .*' She made a ghostly face, and ran off giggling.

Feeling a bit better, Edward walked on up to prep.

Mandy made her way into the kitchen. It was vast, and covered the whole of the basement floor. She wound her way through it to find her mother, who was filling up the enormous dishwasher.

'Sorry, love, I nearly forgot. Tea, two cups, staff sitting room. Do you mind?'

'Sure,' said Mandy. After brewing a pot of tea, she placed two cups and the pot on a heavy silver tray, and took them out into the corridor.

She knew who the tea was for. Lady Anne de la Zouche and Mrs Phipps. Balancing the tray carefully, she came to the end of the long, stuffy passage and paused at the door, ready to knock.

But something made her put her eye to the crack of

the door. Something made her wait, and listen.

Mandy saw through the fug of the the smoky, tatty staffroom that two women were seated in the two most comfortable chairs. Old sofas on which ancient cushions had been carelessly scattered filled up the rest of the room, with ashtrays placed conveniently at hand. Mandy knew that boys were strictly not allowed in, on pain of death, or worse.

Mandy guessed that the better-dressed woman with haughty brown-blonde hair was Lady Anne, and the woman with the frumpy, ill-fitting clothes was Mrs Phipps. There was something wrong about Mrs Phipps – something she couldn't quite place, like looking at a picture that you knew should resolve into something clearer.

There were no other staff members in the room. Lady Anne held a crystal glass full of water in her hand. Mrs Phipps sat immobile, swaying slightly, like a billowing sheet.

'The whelp must be waning,' Mandy heard Lady Anne say. 'I can feel it . . .'

Lady Anne tightened her hand around the glass. Small cracks made their way up the sides. 'I need you to come here, Phipps,' she said.

Mrs Phipps, to Mandy's astonishment, glided across from her seat to Lady Anne, and kneeled in front of her.

Stretching out her hands, Lady Anne placed them on top of Mrs Phipps's head. She breathed, heavily, in long, gasping breaths. Mrs Phipps seemed to shimmer, and to fade, and then, to Mandy's amazement, her body, starting with her head, began to – and there was no other word for it – dissolve. And as Mandy watched, horrified, the body turned into a thick, treacly smoke-like substance, and Lady Anne was breathing it in.

It was all Mandy could do not to drop the tray. It slid in her hands, and she managed to stop a cup falling off. Luckily Lady Anne was too occupied to hear anything.

Then Lady Anne became rigid, and her eyes rolled back in her head, and it felt to Mandy as if she had become a monster, eyeless, faceless, and her body heaved, and heaved, and her head snapped back . . . and then, as horribly as before, a stream of liquid and air gushed out of Lady Anne's mouth and re-formed into Mrs Phipps.

But if that didn't frighten Mandy, what she said next certainly did.

'Pollock . . .'

The two ladies sat, in silence, composed.

Mandy gulped, swallowed her fear and knocked sharply.

'Tea!' said Lady Anne brightly as she came in. 'Thank you!'

Mandy put the tray down, terrified that at any moment they might realise she'd seen them and, as soon as she was dismissed, ran down the corridor. She had to tell Edward what she'd seen. But when? She wouldn't be able to see him until tomorrow. Her mind humming with images, she fled back to the kitchen.

Edward was nearing the main teaching block. He could only think of Mrs Phipps's eyes burning into him, the mysterious figure in the library, and the thing in his bag that was like the Pole dragging a compass needle ever north.

He checked in his pocket for the piece of paper, then thrust his hand into his satchel. It grazed something soft, and strange, and a jolt of terror shook through him. Involuntarily, he yelped. He let go of the object, forcing it back into his bag.

He stopped near a clump of trees, just yards from the form rooms, and dared himself to peek. OK, he said to himself. It can't be anything that strange. What could you find in a library apart from books? He counted to himself. One . . . two . . . three . . . he opened the satchel and looked in.

It was a book. A dark, heavy tome. Something was

compelling him to lift it out, though it was repulsive to the touch, like leather still animated by some force. He wanted to look at it now, where he was, with the trees around him. But he couldn't be discovered outside again. He would have to go into prep. He closed his satchel and continued on to the form rooms.

He looked through the window and saw that the master in charge that night was Mr Bartlett. Edward loathed Mr Bartlett – his red, puffy face, his second-hand, stained tweed suits. He was a pedantic, unimaginative teacher, and he acted as if he was only at Oldstone Manor because he'd fallen on hard times.

Edward noticed that he was reading a newspaper and hoped Bartlett wouldn't notice his arrival. He sidled slowly into the room and took a spare desk quietly. There were some empty ones in the top form room, for those in Eudoky to sit at. He opened the desk and thrust the book into it, slamming the lid shut. The book seemed to be making a noise, scuzzy, fiendish, horrid, low, but nobody else had noticed it. Somebody made a sound, and Bartlett looked up from his copy of *Racing Post*, which he was studying intensely.

'Pollock.'

Edward tensed.

'Out here, please.'

Feeling the eyes of the form room on him, Edward

made his way slowly up to where Bartlett sat, looking at the floor.

'Stand up straight, boy!' said Bartlett. 'Come on, march properly! Not like that! Left right, left right, left right, round the room . . .'

The whole class joined in as Edward marched round the room, his arms out stiffly. Bartlett halted him by his chair. Edward could smell the reek of whisky on him. Bartlett's face was mottled, the veins showing clearly through the skin. Bartlett affected not to notice Edward for a second or two, continuing to read his paper.

'Got a good tip from a stable lad today,' he said, folding the paper and putting it on the desk. 'You're late, aren't you, Pollock?'

Edward looked straight ahead of him.

'Speak up, boy. You're late!'

'Yes, sir!' said Edward.

'Why are you late?'

'Don't know, sir!'

'Well, I suppose we can't all be as special as you. I suppose you think there's a different time scheme in place for you, eh, Pollock?' Bartlett gave him a hefty whack round the shoulder.

'No, sir,' said Edward, to a background of whispering and turning heads. He still felt the noise from the book like a wad of material in his ear.

'Two kappas,' said Bartlett.

Good, thought Edward. I've got away with it. He edged back towards the desk.

'Oh, and Pollock.' Bartlett was stirring in his chair.

'Sir?'

Bartlett had removed his shoes, revealing two red-socked feet. 'Polish these.'

The room erupted into laughter. Edward was seething with hatred.

'Sir, that's not fair!'

'Life isn't fair,' said Bartlett smugly, and pulled two brushes and some polish out of the bottom drawer of his desk. Edward noticed the gleam of a bottle in it before Bartlett slammed it shut.

In front of the whole class Edward polished the shoes, with Bartlett occassionally shouting, 'Faster, boy,' and, 'I can't see my face in them yet.' Eventually they were judged passable and, with another clump round the shoulder, Edward was dismissed.

'Well, get on with your letter now. I'm studying the form for the 3:15 at Fontwell. It's my ticket out of this hellhole.' The boys laughed appreciatively.

'I don't have any paper, sir,' said Edward. He'd left it in the library.

'Well, borrow some.' Bartlett got up, went to the nearest boy who was composing a letter, picked up his pad and tore off three sheets. 'There you go,' he said, tossing them towards Edward. They fluttered to the ground and Edward rushed to pick them up, smiling apologetically at the boy whose paper it was.

Humiliated, Edward went to the desk and tried to write a letter to his parents. But he couldn't even start the standard formula. He couldn't write 'I'm fine'. He wasn't. Not only was he burning with hatred for Bartlett, but he wanted to spill everything out on to the page, to let someone know about the strange figure he'd seen in the library, the book he'd found. The whole day had been so odd, he felt at a loss. If he put his thoughts down on paper, someone might find it and read it. If anything was going on, then he had to be sure who he could trust.

He could feel the book's presence, even through the lid of the desk, as if it were alive, as if it wanted to reach him. He lifted the lid as sneakily as he could to take another look.

'Pollock!' said Mr Bartlett, rustling his paper, and not bothering to look at him. 'I am sure that it is not necessary for you to open and shut your desk every three seconds. Are you writing a letter? Or are you part of some new percussion band?'

The room filled with low laughter. 'No, sir,' said Edward meekly.

71

'Don't do it again, Pollock,' said Bartlett in a lazy sing-song way.

Edward felt in his pockets for a new ink cartridge, came across the piece of paper in his pocket, and pulled it out. He had entirely forgotten about it. He had been distracted by the book. Now it seemed to him as if it might be able to help him – for it had led him to it.

It was old, faded, fragile. He unfolded it carefully and laid it out flat on the desk. It was handwritten, in careful spidery writing, decorated with many curves and tails. He began to decipher it:

What has been hidden will rise up again:
Beware those who seek it for their own gain.
Though the line of the wizard and witch is strong,
A pure one will find it, not one who seeks wrong.
The blood of a maiden must surely be spilled,
For the source of evil to be truly killed;
Lest words of nightmare and terror are spoken,
And the wall between ghost and man is broken.

It made very little sense to him. But it brought back the nightmare he had had that morning, which had come from the gloomiest, rockiest recesses of his mind. It brought back the feeling he had had when he had laid the raven on the monument. Perhaps the wall is already broken, he thought, thinking of the figure he had seen in the library . . . He shuddered. Maybe, he thought, if I think about something else I'll be able to solve it. He filled up his pen with the cartridge, and tried to start his letter.

As prep dragged on, he ached to look at the book. Every time he unfolded and reread the poem, it made less sense to him, until it was like reading meaningless sounds. The bell boy finally left the room and Edward watched him sprinting down to where the bell hung. He rang it ferociously and the boys all started clattering and putting away their things. Edward carefully folded up the poem and put it back in his pocket. Eudoky had a bit of free time before they had to go up to the dorms, and his punishment had been forgotten.

Edward lifted the lid of the desk, and took out the book. It felt cold now, and less horrific. He held it close to his side. He didn't want to put it in his satchel; he felt that he needed to keep it in sight. Bartlett was still immersed in his paper, not having quite got up the strength to stumble down to the staffroom for his evening whisky. Edward sidled out of the room, trying not to let anyone see what he was carrying. It was far too conspicuous. It looked like he'd stolen it from the locked cabinets in the library. He couldn't pass it off as a tatty old textbook.

He'd made it out of the form room when Mr Bartlett called out, 'Po-llock! PO-LLOCK!'

Edward halted, rocked back on his heels, and turned round.

'What's that you've got there?' asked Bartlett, huffily.

Sudden alarm filled him.

'A book, sir,' he said.

'No, Pollock, I can see that you are carrying a book. Most people could see that. Even some of these imbeciles here.' He indicated the dispersing boys with a languid hand.

Edward looked blankly at Bartlett.

'In your other hand, idiot!'

He looked blindly at his hand.

'Your letter, nitwit! You haven't handed in your letter! How can I check it if you don't hand it in?' He harrumphed. 'Are you hiding something?'

'No, sir,' said Edward, immensely relieved.

Bartlett looked disappointed. Edward ran to him and thrust the letter into his hands, dashing out before he could say anything else.

The clock was striking seven as Edward made his way up the stairs and into the dorms. His dorm was one of six on the first floor of the Manor, on the same level as the library. Everybody else had gone out to play cricket in the nets, or to play tennis or just relax on the grass.

Upstairs in the Manor the dormitory was quiet and still, all the beds made, all the chairs tidy. Edward's bed was in an alcove by the window, overlooking the court-yard below, and further beyond, the lush greens and blues of the valley. The window seat was a haven for him, and he would often sit there and absorb the light or listen to the river when there was nobody else around. It proved useful at night as well, as he'd sit there in the dark, with a torch, and read. The curtains were so thick and old – probably left over from the war, when they had been blackout curtains – that they kept the light out, and thanks to them Edward had not yet been caught.

Edward settled on his bed. He breathed in the calm of the warm room. Carefully, he lay the book on the duvet. It looked so strange, sitting on the familiar tex-ture of his bedcovers.

When he reached out to touch it, it seemed to him as if the book was giving off heat. Delicately, he just brushed its surface, and then recoiled. It was covered in little hairs – like a nettle, or a spider. He held up his hand to see if he'd been stung – and then relaxed. How could a book hurt him?

With more resolve, he carefully gripped hold of the

cover with one forefinger and one thumb. And a delicious sense started to spread up from his finger, all the way up his arm and into his brain. He could hear, at the edge of sound, voices whispering. The sensation gripped hold of his brain. It was pleasure, but with a sharpness he had never felt before, something that was so beyond any experience he had had that he could not name it. He felt his eyes close, against his will, and began to lift the cover of the book . . .

'BUUUUNDDDDLE!' shouted someone. Three of his dorm-mates came rushing in – Munro, Murdoch and Peake. They bundled themselves on top of him, everyone kicked and shoved and pushed for a bit, then Edward heaved from the bottom and toppled over the whole pile.

'What are you doing?' said Edward, hastily thrusting the book under his pillow.

There was silence for a moment as everyone caught their breaths. 'I can't breathe . . . I can't breathe!' shouted Munro, and began faking a choking attack on the floor.

'The nets are all full,' said Peake, elbowing Murdoch.

'What's the point, Peake?' said Murdoch. 'Why did you do that?'

'Do what?' said Peake, and shrugged his shoulders mysteriously.

'Look, you've made me bleed!' said Murdoch.

Munro stopped his choking. 'What?'

'Well, somebody's been bleeding. Look at this!' Murdoch pointed to Edward's duvet cover. There was a small bloodstain on it.

Edward looked at his hands, and there where he had gripped the book was a vivid, bloody pinprick. 'It's me,' said Edward. 'But it's OK. Anyway, I'm trying to read!' He kicked the last bit of Peake on to the floor, who slid off the bed and put all his weight on to his arms, collapsing on to the carpet, making a noise like a pack of rabid dogs.

All peace had been disrupted. Peake, Munro and Murdoch stayed in the dorm until everyone else had come in from the nets, as cheerily and noisily as usual. They all undressed and brushed their teeth at the cracked and stained sink. Mrs Ferrers, mouse-like, came round to tuck them in.

'Don't forget to change your pants and socks,' she said. 'That means you, Munro. And Peake, why you can never remember to pin your socks together, I don't know. Go and do it now.'

After Peake had slunk out and slunk back in again, and the boys were finally settled, and Mrs Ferrers had told them all what frightful little monsters they were, she said goodnight and set off to her tiny flat.

O'Brien was on duty that night, and he came in now, holding a clipboard. 'Now, boys,' he said. 'I want you all to sleeeep,' drawing out the 'ee'. 'Sleeep is a tonic. It is nature's marvellous medicine, to make your brains all ready and raring to go in the morning. Sleeep.'

'He sounds like the Wicked Witch,' whispered Edward to Munro. 'He's probably making flying monkeys in the labs!' Munro giggled.

'I want everybody to drop off as soon as his head hits the pillow,' O'Brien said, marching up and down the dormitory, muttering his lecture, waiting until he was sure everyone was settled. Soon all was quiet, and O'Brien slipped out. The light on the landing cast one last orange bar on to the floor before it was clicked off, and the room was in darkness.

Edward waited for an hour by his watch. He had to be absolutely sure that no one in the dorm would be awake to question him. He sat up in bed, as carefully as he could. If he got up too quickly, he risked making a loud noise that would wake everyone instantly. If, on the other hand, he raised himself more slowly, then the creaking of the ancient bedsprings would be extended. The decision was made for him, as he bolted at a movement from the bed next to him, and scrambled on to the window seat, pulling the curtains tightly shut behind him.

The window seat gave a tremendous whine as he settled down on to it. He sat stock-still for a minute or so, as if concrete had been poured into his limbs and set solid. Not a sound came from the dorm.

Edward fitted his back into the corner, settling into the soft cushion. To feel Oldstone Manor behind and beneath him was comforting. He let his mind wander, and he thought of all the other people who had sat here, in years and centuries gone by. They too had gazed across the valley, or been absorbed in a book. He wondered what they had thought, how they had felt. Did they feel the scored lines of the stone in their back? Did they see the fat, bright moon casting a ghost-light across the valley, and dream of strange, dark things in the night?

His reveries were interrupted by the book he was holding gingerly in his hands. It seemed to be calling to him.

The quiet rustle of the trees made a scratchy accompaniment to the gauzy lapping of the river. The big oak tree that stood by the pond stretched its arms out benevolently towards Edward.

He trembled a little, feeling that every movement he was making was magnified a hundred times. He weighed the book in his hands. His breath was coming unevenly. The book seemed a lot heavier now that he was still. Its blackness was inviting. It was telling him that he would not need his senses, that it would immerse him, make him disappear. Astronauts must feel like that when they stood on the edge of the sky.

He set the book down on the seat, since it was now too heavy to hold, and was making his wrists ache. He studied the cover. It was pitch-black, with no title or design on it.

As he opened it, the dark matter of the universe shifted. Even if he had been able to stop reading, his doom had already been chosen for him, the black threads of his fate already woven.

Around the edges of the frontispiece was a curious design, that looked like Ms and Vs intertwined, each loose end sprouting into patterns. There was a picture in the front, the like of which he had never seen. It was so delicately, so finely drawn, that every feature seemed to live, every leaf had energy, every letter had grace.

A man and a woman were drawn on either side of the page. They were split by the thin trunk of a tree, but they were joined together by a line which looped from head to head and heart to heart. They were both dressed in long, flowing robes, which seemed to blow and shimmer even as Edward watched. Their expressions were neutral, but had an air of mystical serenity that filled Edward as he gazed at them. The pair stood on top of a mountain, and beneath them spread what looked like the whole world. In each corner of the page were drawn figures. Judging by their attributes, Edward thought they represented the four elements of earth, air, fire and water.

The picture seemed to move, and live, and Edward came closer to it, the details becoming clearer and clearer. At first he saw the dark curls of the man's hair, the purple richness of his robe. His hand lay on the head of a black dog, that twisted its neck up to look at its master. He saw the woman's slender, elegant hands, with jewels more prized than kingdoms, sapphires as deep blue as where the whales dwell, emeralds that sang of jungles. Neither man nor woman acknowledged him, and he felt their presence as a troubling sensation – that of great calm and benignity which could swiftly turn wild and savage.

Then the perspective lengthened, and he saw whole cities rise and fall beneath the gaze of the man and the woman; he saw the rise of civilisation, of beauty and grace, and he saw that everything was good beneath them. And then he saw creatures massing together, making low, wailing noises, and they seemed to scratch at an invisible barrier around the bright world of the man and the woman.

These creatures roamed the barrier, calling, raving,

scratching, slobbering. The rustling sound they made filled Edward with horror and he turned over the page. His heart fluttered within him, and he felt sick, the bile rising up in him, scorching his throat. There were letters on the page. But the book was not in English. It was not in French, or Latin, or Greek, or any other language that he could ever hope to decipher. It didn't look like the Arabic script that he had seen among his father's books, or the Japanese pictograms on the paintings in the music room. It was a symbol language that seemed harsh and brutal. As his eyes went across the page the sickness in him grew, and he felt dizzy.

He saw on the page, as if it were real, a knight in gilded armour. He was mounted on a grey horse, with green and gold caparisons. The knight had his helm off. He had tousled hair so black it was almost purple, and thoughtful eyes. He looked familiar, but Edward couldn't place him. The knight smiled at him and started to speak, but Edward did not understand him. When the knight realised this, he began to ride his horse up and down, nervously. Then Edward became worried, because the knight had put his helm on and set his lance, and began to gallop towards him, the lance pointing directly at his chest.

Then something happened. Some instinct rose up in Edward and overwhelmed him. He heard the knight shouting something, but it was so faint he could not make out the words. And now all sorts of images were flashing across his eyes. Fragments of his subconscious were being worked out on the page in front of him – images that fitted together, that seemed to make sense, to connect – the raven morphed into a dog, which changed into a boy. He relaxed, and let the images flow.

Then he began to notice that with each passing vision, something was going wrong. Everything took on a distorted quality. If people spoke they spoke slowly, sinisterly, like a tape going backwards. Then people appeared with heads growing out of their stomachs, with teeth in the palms of their hands, and they were all crowding around, rushing, laughing, dancing and wailing, and among them was one who was taller than all the rest, and it saw Edward, and he felt its dark presence. It approached Edward and stood barely a foot away. It was shrouded in a long cloak so that he could not make out any features, and when it spoke Edward quailed at the sound.

The thing asked him what he desired, and Edward found that he was spilling forth everything that he had ever held in check, every nasty, mean thought that he had suppressed or forgotten about. The creature held him by the neck, Edward closed his eyes to try and shut it out but it pressed his eyelids open and Edward began to see things that he never thought could be, had never thought existed. Still the creature pushed at Edward, asking him what he wanted. The sight of Imp killing the raven passed across his mind, and the creature laughed. Edward fought, and hit, and shouted and roared, but still the creature held him to the images that burned and raced before him. He tried to stop them, with every straining, shivering sinew in his body, he tried, but there was nothing he could do. He began to weaken, and he felt cold, and broken.

Mrs Ferrers was on her rounds the next morning, at seven o'clock, patiently going round the dorms in the Manor waking everyone up. The day was bright and clear. She came to Edward's dormitory, and burst in.

'Wakey wakey, rise and shine!' she said, and pulled open the nearest pair of curtains. Boys stirred and mumbled. Mrs Ferrers looked around. Edward was not in his bed. Sometimes he got up early to practise the piano in the music school, so she was not too bothered. She went over to the next set of windows, joshing the boys who were still in bed. She yanked the curtains open, and stepped back with a gasp. Edward was lying there on the window seat, pale as an Elizabethan nobleman powdered with arsenic. It took three boys shaking him before he woke up.

The first thing he saw was Mrs Ferrers's kind face. 'My dear boy,' she said. 'Are you all right?'

Edward nodded slowly. Then he realised that he was missing something. He scrabbled around on the window seat. The book had vanished.

Four

'hy did you do it?' Mrs Ferrers asked Edward, with concern in her voice as she put a thermometer in his mouth. Edward had got dressed, and was sitting in the matron's room, balanced on a little wooden stool.

'I wanted to see how long I could stay awake,' he said, screwing up his left eye slightly. It seemed a sensible answer, in the circumstances, and she accepted it, with much shaking of her head and tutting.

'What a silly boy. You should think about what you're doing before you do it. You're off games for the day.'

Edward usually longed to be off games, so he was ecstatic, even if he was feeling a bit shaky and spooked. The loathsome things that he had seen in the book kept coming back to him, and the memory of the knight kept galloping into his thoughts, all mixed up with the boy in the Hall in his dream. On top of all this, he felt thinned, spread out, as if his body had somehow been stretched; the leathery taste of the book was constantly at the back of his throat. It seemed to him like the anxiety that you feel when you're walking home at night in the dark and you *know* that there's something behind you.

'Go on now, off to breakfast,' said Mrs Ferrers. 'Make sure you eat enough.'

'OK,' said Edward, and slipped down the back stairs into Kakophagy, where breakfast had already started. He felt distanced from everyone else, and could not join in with the banter; he thought he noticed people looking at him differently, and wondered if he was getting paranoid. He looked at himself in the back of a spoon and noticed that he was still deathly pale. The book has disappeared, he thought. What has happened to it? It was troubling him, greatly.

After the meal, he sought out Will Strangore as they and the other scholars filed down to Eudoky. It was sluggish, and there was an overripe feeling in the air.

'You're goddamned quiet,' said Strangore. (He had been reading Ernest Hemingway.) 'Have you forgotten there's a Latin test?'

'Hm? On what?'

'Gerunds.'

'Score,' said Edward, with an air of cavalier distraction.

'Are you all right?' asked Will.

Edward paused, wondering what he could possibly say to him. 'Listen . . . I want to tell you something . . . I don't know, this weird thing happened and I think it's got something to do with Lady Anne.'

Lane Glover came past the other way, his hands hanging loosely, his school shorts worn as low as he dared. He heard Edward, and came closer.

'Wassup, homeboys,' he said. 'What are you talking about?'

'Nothing,' said Edward.

Lane Glover launched himself at Will, pushing him on to the ground.

'Hey!' said Edward. 'Stop picking on him!'

'Why? He's such a weakling.' Guy pushed Will as he was trying to get up again. Will's hand scraped against the ground. Edward pulled him up.

'I heard you say Lady Anne's name. Don't like her, do you? Think she'll get rid of your favourite Fraser?'

'Go away, Glover,' said Edward.

'Fine,' said Glover. 'I don't care anyway.' He went on up to lessons.

Edward would usually have let fly with a volley of

considered insults, but this time his mind was else-where.

Will looked very calm. He tended to bottle up his feelings. Edward knew better than to say anything, but all the same he patted his cousin on the shoulder and smiled at him. He could feel Will's hatred of Glover. But there were other, more pressing things to talk about.

This is useless, he thought. I'll have to tell Will about the book or I'll burst. He turned to his cousin as they entered Eudoky. There were about twenty minutes before lessons.

'What would you say,' said Edward, as he felt in his ink-blotted wooden desk for his tattered Latin books, 'if something weird had happened to me? Like . . . you know, when I was younger and I thought I saw spirits in the forests.'

'Oh yeah, when you went loony.'

The way he said it was hurtful to Edward, for the memory of it was still fresh and vivid. It had been when he'd first arrived at Oldstone Manor. He had tried to share it with Will, but he hadn't believed him, and Edward had kept the sense of awe it had given him secret ever since. It was the only other – he didn't want to say it, but it was the only word he could think of to describe it – supernatural experience which he could remember having, and he had felt it had connected him to the Manor in a way which other boys could not understand.

Edward remembered the time when the two of them had been playing camps. He had been standing guard over the entrance to the camp which Strangore and he had built together. They had called it, for reasons not clear to either of them, Temple.

It was at the north end of the woods, far away from the school, right at the edge of the mysterious zone known as Out-Of-Bounds. He had been holding a stick against his shoulder – except of course in his imagination it wasn't a stick, it was a spear. He was by turns a Roman guard, marching up and down Hadrian's Wall, or outside Caesar's Palace, then a Persian guarding the tent of Alexander in the savage lands of Bactria. His arm had ached, but he hadn't minded. Soldiers had to endure pain.

Edward had felt that here he was at the edge of the infinite. Hardly anything moved except his heart, and the things that did move, moved in sympathy with it. A few twigs crackled in the wind. Beech trees nodded gracefully. A little bird walked upside down under a branch. He had emptied his mind of noise, and had allowed the forest to pour into it. He remembered that he had been able to see it in its exact details, even when his eyes were shut. He recalled that everything had felt porous, as if he could have merged with everything else, or crossed over into a place that was not this world.

It was then that he thought he had seen the spirits of the wood. The trees around him had seemed to grow and move, to become animated beings with old, cruel, sad thoughts. For a few moments he had felt linked into their minds, and it was profoundly different. He felt the whole earth beneath him swarming with life, he felt insignificant, he felt humble.

This feeling, that he was nothing but another growth in the forest of the world, was what brought the young Edward Pollock to the attention of the melancholy pair of eyes that had watched him ever since. It was then that he had been chosen.

Edward remembered how Strangore had come back from the mission he'd been on, had broken something, some connection – Edward was sure he heard something snap in his mind – and Edward was not part of the forest any more, and the sense of the wood spirits vanished. He told Strangore excitedly what he'd seen, but it sounded wrong, and Will had looked at Edward in his owlish way and shaken his head.

Since then Edward had often thought about what he'd seen. He'd even gone back into the woods on his own but, however hard he tried, he never saw the spirits again. He knew that the experience had brought him closer to Oldstone Manor. And he also felt as if he had been touched by something outlandish, and it was something secret, which from that moment onwards he had decided to keep to himself.

That was why he did not like Will's tone, and why he hesitated now to tell him about the book. It made him feel exposed, vulnerable. But he needed help, and Will was the only person he could think of to whom he could turn. And now at least he had evidence, which might persuade his scientifically-minded cousin. The piece of paper with the poem on it.

'Come on, you can tell me,' said Will, not unkindly. He saw that there was an intensity in Edward's face which meant that something was at stake.

Edward told Will, hesitantly at first, everything that had happened. He had carefully folded the piece of paper and put it in his pocket, and he pulled it out now.

Will took it from him.

'Well, it *looks* genuine enough,' he said.

'You mean you'd think I'd *make* something like that?' said Edward, outraged.

'I wouldn't put it past you, if you had a reason for it.' Will held it out of Edward's reach, and read it over. When he had finished it, he read it again.

'So what d'you think?' said Edward, at last.

'Doesn't mean anything to me,' said Strangore. 'Tell me more.'

'We'll have to go upstairs.' Edward led him to the library, where he had left *Idylls of the King*, and showed him its green and gold bindings.

'You found the poem in this?' said Strangore.

'Yes.'

'I wonder why. Maybe it's meant as a clue. What else is there?

'Will,' said Edward. He breathed in deeply. He didn't want to sound strange. 'I think . . .' and for a moment he didn't know how to start. 'I think something dark's going on. Last night, I heard voices on the drive. Lady Anne and her friend, talking. I heard her saying that all the signs were pointing here.'

'She probably meant motorway signs,' said Strangore, and slapped his thigh.

'Will! Listen! Lady Anne is here to find something. I'm sure of it!' He hesitated for a moment before adding, 'And I found this . . . strange book . . . and when I opened it . . .'

'But where is this book?'

Edward shrugged. 'I don't know. It's . . . vanished.' He didn't want to say just yet that he suspected that somehow the book had been absorbed into his mind, that even now he felt it stirring within him, stretching and pressing against his skull. 'But I think that this poem might have something to do with it.'

Strangore laughed. 'Well, let's look at it again.'

The two boys bent over the piece of paper, and Strangore shook his head. 'Beats me. *The blood of a maiden must surely be spilled*. Well, that's all right, it can't be either of us. We're not maidens.'

'No,' said Edward. But something he had read about Galahad flashed in the furrows of his mind, like a gold cup turned over by a plouging team of oxen. And then before the memory surfaced, it vanished again.

Will finished reading the poem and looked up. 'Right. Anything else you need to tell me?' he said.

'Oh . . .' Edward hesitated, and then he told Strangore about the grave and the raven.

'Now that is interesting,' said Will. 'How long till lessons?'

Edward looked at his watch. 'Ten minutes.'

'Good. I'm just going to check it out. I'll see you later.'

'Later,' said Edward.

When Will had left, Edward went to the other side of the library and looked out of the window into the courtyard. Mandy was there.

'Skiving off school?' he shouted at her.

'No,' said Mandy. 'I'm ill.' She coughed unconvincingly. 'Edward, I've been looking all over for you. Come down. I need to tell you something!'

Edward set off excitedly through the library and down the back stairs. These stairs led into a no-man's-land of clutter: discarded trunks, ancient wicker laundry baskets; past rooms whose use had been forgotten – sculleries, butteries, pantries and storehouses – through a twisty maze of tunnels and finally into Kakophagy. Edward pattered down the stairs, wondering what it was that Mandy could have found out.

The ancient smells of the kitchen hung around heavily, speaking of the lunches of centuries ago, when the boys could drink beer and subsisted almost entirely on bread and cheese. Edward came into a corridor by the kitchen, where the cold rooms were. He thought he saw Mandy just ahead of him.

'Mandy!' he said.

'In here!' she replied, darting into one of the rooms. There was an uncomfortable, grinding feeling in his mind, a sunken humming, which he couldn't get rid of.

'Come on, Edward,' said Mandy.

He followed her into the cold room.

'What's up, Mandy?' he said, looking at her back. The door to the cold room closed itself. It was hard to see. Vapours rose off from everywhere, and it was

95

deadly silent. 'Hang on,' he said, and turned back to open it. But it was stuck. 'What's wrong with this thing? Hey, Mandy, come and help me.' He turned round. Mandy was still standing with her back to him. 'Mandy?' She did not reply. He let go of the door handle. His body tensed. He noticed that all around him hung bloodied carcasses. They swung eerily. Crates of frozen fishfingers, burgers, peas were stacked around. Edward felt a freezing tingle seep up his body from the small of his back to his neck. 'Mandy?' He went up to her and touched her shoulder. It was very cold. She still did not turn round.

'Mandy!' He shook her, and she dissolved and in her place was a stack of ice cubes which began to tumble down to the ground.

'What the hell!' Edward, terrified, rushed back to the door. 'Help! Let me out!' The ice cubes were reassembling themselves, forming into something. He rattled the door handle. 'Is anyone there?'

The ice cubes had taken shape now, becoming an indistinct creature, a faceless, humanoid thing, that slowly moved towards Edward, two arm-like extensions held out in front of it. A crushing sense of claustrophobia enveloped Edward. There was no way out. Frantic, frazzled, he backed up against the door. The carcasses around him shook and shimmered, and he noticed again how bloody they were, and how, in the half-light, they looked like human bodies.

'Help!' Edward's breath made smoky shapes in the air. He was growing more desperate, and the chattering and squealing in his mind was getting louder. He shook the door, and the thing came closer. Edward saw his hands turning blue, and icicles growing on his clothes.

The fiend's arctic outstretched arms touched him, and the cold spread from its fingertips, into Edward, and Edward could feel it entering into the pith and marrow of his body, freezing his sinews and his blood . . .

Something was fighting in him and he felt power surge from his mind; his body filled as if with liquid strength, and he turned to face the monstrous icy form which was now engulfing him in permafrost.

He grabbed hold of the thing by what could only be its neck, and he felt the warmth flow out of him and it was thrown backwards.

But whatever it was, it had strength too, and it gathered all the frozen air in the room to it and advanced once more on Edward. He felt the cold of deepest space pour into him, and he began to slump. He felt himself being picked up, being raised to one of the hooks that hung from the ceiling, and still he fought, but whatever strength of will was in him had faded . . . He felt his eyelids beginning to stick together, and his fingers curling up.

Yet, as his consciousness ebbed away, he thought he saw a face forming in the ice.

Five

dward's brain was slowing down. Thoughts were difficult. Even fear had disappeared as his heartbeat got slower and slower. So this is what death is like, he thought. No white lights, no feeling of peace, just emptiness.

The thing sniffed. But it didn't close in on him. A sliver of hope began to form in Edward's mind. Why wasn't it finishing him off? He felt a scuttling in his mind again.

Once more, the fiendish creature sniffed all over him. But then it let out a wail of disappointment, and Edward was dropped on to the floor. As quickly as it had formed together, the thing dispersed back into hundreds of scattered ice cubes. Edward's breaths came in tiny, ragged gasps. He was stiff, a dead weight. He couldn't move.

The door opened, and one of the cooks came in. He made towards a pile of boxes, and then noticed Edward lying on the floor.

'Clear off!' said the cook. 'You're not meant to be in here!'

Edward just about managed to lift up an arm.

'Hey . . . you all right, son?' The cook bent down. 'Bloody hell, you're frozen! Here, hold on a second.' The cook dragged him out into the corridor, stood for a moment looking at him, then turned abruptly. Shortly he came rushing back with another man. The two picked Edward up as if he were a hind that had just been shot, and carried him up the back stairs and into the library, laying him out on the sofa. The cook went to get Mrs Ferrers, and the other man stayed with Edward.

'Where do you sleep, son?' he said, but Edward could not answer.

Downstairs, the handle of the cold-room door moved, and somebody slipped out, and walked unnoticed away.

Mrs Ferrers came into the library and rushed up to Edward, who was purple with cold.

'My dear boy! What have you been doing!'

'N-n-nothing, Mrs Ferrers.'

'I'll have to take your temperature.' She flitted out,

and was back again in an instant, forcing it between Edward's teeth. 'Way below normal. You should stay away from lessons. I'll put a note on the noticeboard. You'd better go up to bed. Will you two carry him? He's in the west dormitory.'

The two men took Edward to his dorm, and laid him gently on his bed. Mrs Ferrers followed them.

'You stay here, and don't move for the rest of the day. OK?' She pressed his forehead.

Edward couldn't quite believe what had happened. His mind was tumbling with fear. Mrs Ferrers left him curled up under his duvet, and then later brought a tray of food. He didn't touch it, and she sat by him gently coercing him until he managed to eat half a shepherd's pie. 'Good boy,' she said. By then Edward was feeling better. He started to read something, and after a while he found that he could move without worrying that his finger would break off because it was frozen. Soon he had relaxed entirely.

After lunch Strangore came up to see him.

'How you doing?' he said. 'What happened to you?'

'I was attacked by an ice monster,' said Edward in an undertone.

'What?' said Will.

'I was attacked! By a monster! Made of ice!' said Edward, more emphatically.

'Oh come off it, Ed,' said Will, affectionately. He was worried about his friend.

'Never mind,' said Edward. He could see that he wasn't going to make Will believe him.

'Now listen,' said Will. 'I went down to the churchyard and looked at the grave you put the raven on. There's a pattern round the edge of it, of Ms and Vs. What d'you think it could mean?'

'I don't know.' Edward pulled the blanket round him tighter.

'Look, I've got to go, it's lessons. But work on it.'

Edward picked up his copy of *Idylls of the King* and leafed through it, until he came to the story of Merlin and Vivien.

Merlin and Vivien . . . he knew the story, that Vivien had locked Merlin in an oak tree, having taken all his power from him. He had always wondered what had happened to Merlin afterwards. To have had all the magic in the world at your command, and then to have it taken away, to become a shrunken, helpless shell . . . Merlin's nightmares must have been terrifying, thought Edward.

He found himself drifting into sleep. Ms and Vs . . . He slept, and he dreamed of the two people he had seen in the front of the book, and the power they had wielded over the ages: the balance they trod between good and evil, combining both in the creation and destruction of the universe.

Later in the day, the sun, which was burning his left cheek pleasantly, woke Edward up. He lay on his back, and stared into space. The dormitory around him was, in its ordinariness and familiarity, a place of safety. The football posters and cartoon-character duvets were normal, reassuring presences. The things he had seen, in the black book and in the cold room, had crawled into the back of his consciousness. He felt a little better. But there was still the mysterious disappearance of the book to deal with. Where had it gone? he wondered. He had held it the night before, but now . . .

It had dematerialised. There was absolutely no sign of it around his bed. He looked at the window seat where he had sat, and grubbed around on the floor. But there was nothing there. Things don't just disappear into thin air, he thought. He knew that. Or at least he'd thought he'd known. Until he had seen the ice creature.

He wondered whether the book had gone back to the library where the mysterious figure had put it. He got up and shuffled his way there through the corridors. It was deserted. The room was as it always had been. He went to the place where he had first found the black book – but there was nothing there. A sense of distress gripping him, he looked on all the shelves around it, and then further afield – but nothing came up.

The thought that had been occupying him now came forward. He was desperately hoping that it wasn't true; that the book had, by some strange osmosis, absorbed itself into his brain. Once more he checked under the shelves, behind the radiators. Frustrated, he sat down on the sofa.

It must be true, he thought. Somehow . . . it is inside me. The frightful thought compelled him to look out of the window, to seek what was safe and commonplace. For the first time now he realised that what was clamouring inside him, shrieking in its unknowable, icy language, must be the black book. In order to try to suppress it, he focused his attention on what was going on below.

The school was particularly busy today, getting ready for a drinks party to welcome the benefactors, and Edward was quite relieved to be out of it all. Tables had to be moved, chairs found, marquees put up and form rooms tidied, masters dusted off, boys cleaned, Norman loos unblocked and the special secret staff loo filled with flowers and smelly soaps.

Edward watched masters, kitchen staff and boys all flapping about anxiously. He sensed nervous laughter bubbling under the surface. A drinks table was being set up in the courtyard, with bowls of enticing-looking liquids placed all along its white length, interspersed with piles of fruits and mini-sandwiches still fresh under clingfilmed bubbles. It was all carried off with clinical precision. The kitchen girls, Mandy among them, in their white gloves, hats and aprons, were like doctors as they laid out the cold meats on the white slab of the table.

Looking down at them, Edward watched who he hoped was the real Mandy carry out her tasks, joking and laughing with her mother. She put down a plate of sandwiches and looked directly up at him. That has to be her, he thought.

Then something curious happened. Edward shuddered as a ghost-light splashed over the scene. The walls of his brain seemed to be thinning. A darkness encroached, and he saw his own body, lying spread-eagled on a table, and a shadowy figure bent over him. He held his head and shook it, trying to force his sight back to normal, and when he looked up again the vision had gone.

Edward was disturbed, frightened. All around him, what he had thought of as the safe boundaries of his world were being infiltrated by sinister presences. How could I ever have felt safe in Oldstone Manor? he thought. He considered the meaning of what he had just seen, but could reach for no explanation. Exasperated, he left the window. Perhaps the book is trying to tell me something, he thought. He felt hungry to have it back in its hands, away from his mind. A hunger that felt like it couldn't ever be satisfied. He picked up a novel – one he'd read before – and was soon immersed in it.

He didn't notice the time passing, and it was almost five o'clock when he looked up – time for Bartlett to take roll call. Edward heard him stumbling up the stone stairs, muttering to himself. He reeled into the library. A mixture of the boot room, the staff smoking-room and alcohol came before him.

'Evenin', Eddy my boy,' he said gruffly. Edward winced at the familiarity. Not even his parents called him Eddy. Bartlett clasped him by the shoulder. 'You'd better run along to your dorm. Tell the chaps that Bartlett'll be along in a minute. *Cave* and all that!' He cupped his hands around his mouth and bellowed, '*CAAY-VEEY!*'

Edward shuffled back to the dorms. He was only too glad to be away from Bartlett, whose teeth looked as if a demented toddler had rearranged them. His nostril hair glared out angrily from his nasal cavity, merging into what Bartlett liked to think of as his military moustache.

Bartlett rolled into the dorm like a sailor. 'Ah, my boys,' he said. His spittle arched through the air. He was breathing heavily, and leant against the washbasin. Edward hoped for a second that it would break under his weight. 'Roll call, old chaps. Now, no shenan-in-ani . . . I mean peccadill-peccadilly . . . now behave yourselves, old boys. Especially you.' He pointed. '*Pollock*,' he said.

Oh no, thought Edward.

'Pollock,' he said. 'Come out here, Pollock. Out into the middle of the dorm. Come on.'

He walked out, slowly. Everyone in the dorm was looking. He stood near to Bartlett and fixed his eyes on the ground.

'Pollock, my dear boy. I have an important question to ask you.'

'What is it, sir?' asked Edward, hoping that it would be something about subjunctives or Tennyson.

'Have you ever known what it is to love a woman?' he said, with the air of a tutor in the arts of love. Edward felt fire in his cheeks. All the boys laughed.

'Do you know, my dear, dear boy,' he continued, 'what the love of a woman can be? How it can . . .' Here he staggered, and clutched at the washstand to save himself. 'How it can make you feel like . . . well, like nothing Tennyson could ever talk about, with his mystical mumbo-jumbo. He didn't know what it was like, eh, Pollock?' He looked around at the dorm. 'Pollock,' he said, 'Pollock is a man of the world. Aren't you, Pollock?'

Edward was squirming.

'Well, Pollock?'

He didn't answer. Bartlett sighed in disappointment. 'Well, Pollock. I gather from your silence . . . from your intransigence . . . from your intractability . . . that you're not at all as worldly as I thought. I suppose you've never snatched a kiss from the delightful Mandy in the kitchens? That you've never walked, hand in hand, down to the river bank and gazed at the moon?'

His red face was taking up all Edward's vision. His scratchy tweed jacket, stained with a multitude of sins, was repulsive. He could smell everywhere Bartlett'd been, no doubt in the last few years.

'Tell the dormitory, Pollock! Tell these assembled youths of your first love! Tell them of that first kiss, snatched behind the tree. Tell the world!'

Edward's eyes were burning. He pushed away from Bartlett as violently as he could. Every single boy in the dorm was giggling, guffawing, bellowing. He sensed inevitability, a ball rolling into its accustomed furrow, mechanisms falling into place. The world had slowed down. Why did it feel like he had seen this before? He sensed a balance tipping over.

He tried to laugh, tried to pretend that he didn't care. But he couldn't hide the hatred, the fact that he despised Bartlett as a monster, a foul, slime-encrusted beast who had desecrated something. 'Monster,' he muttered, under his breath.

Suddenly Bartlett looked ridiculous and Edward relaxed. But he felt the presence in his mind tighten itself. Mrs Ferrers came in. 'Come on, then, everyone,' she said, and Bartlett loped off like a toothless wolf.

Six

dward threw himself on his bed and looked at the enormous pile of books on his chair. Milo was still balancing on top of them. At least, he thought, there was still something constant in his life. As he lay there, he considered what had happened that day. He didn't think that the book was a hallucination, or a dream, or anything like that, feeling it as he did in his mind, in his very cells. It wasn't just a distortion of reality created by his brain. It had come from something outside of him.

Whatever it was, it was extremely powerful. What he'd felt in the cold room had wrenched his nerves, fired his adrenalin like nothing ever before. And last night when he had opened the book he felt as if he'd opened a gateway into all the mysteries of the universe. And then there was the face in the ice, which he was sure he'd seen somewhere before . . .

There was the drinks party, he thought. It was a good opportunity to study Lady Anne – he might be able to glean some information if he watched her whilst she didn't think she was being watched. She might let something slip to Mrs Phipps of her intentions. He was feeling better – the sleep and the novel had restored him – and he decided to take the initiative and go down to the courtyard. He could hide behind a screen of bushes and watch what was going on.

Mrs Ferrers had bustled off, more elegant than usual in a grey dress, and the boys were all calm, lying on their beds, reading, or playing pencil cricket. Edward stretched casually, and for just a second too long. His neighbour Munro looked up at him.

'Where are you going, Pollock?'

'Loo,' he said.

The bathroom was full of echoes and dripping noises. He shut the door loudly, to make it seem as if he'd gone in, but stayed on the outside. He had to keep the fiction up in case anyone came in and asked where he was. He knew which floorboards creaked in the corridor, and tried to avoid the noisiest places. At one point he had to edge along the skirting board, clinging to the walls. He made it without making too much noise, and crept down the back stairs.

Avoiding the flitting figures of the kitchen girls, he sneaked through the passageways and found a door that led on to the courtyard. It was right in the corner, and almost hidden by a group of shrubs – ideal for his purposes. The sense of being on a mission, of actively seeking out clues, swelled him with action. He nipped out of the door and ducked down. He could see, clearly, most of the courtyard.

The jazz band had struck up. He could hear the murmur of the voices too – a small lake of wafflings, boastings and whisperings. The band darted knives through the chatter. He crept to his favourite corner and listened.

In the sun the courtyard looked like the inside of a honey pot. Edward had a sudden image of the guests as delirious bees, eager to get at their share. He noticed Lady Anne and Mrs Phipps standing in one corner. Mrs Phipps did not say very much, only responding shortly to questions from the little group of people around Lady Anne. Mr Fraser and an old lady were standing nearer to Edward.

He leant in closer, listening to the bubbles of conversation, allowing them to pop and burst pleasurably in his ears. Lady Anne had not engaged with anyone yet. Now was the time when she might let something slip to Phipps.

'And how is the new music school coming along?' said the old lady, impossibly refined, who was standing near him.

'It's a computer room, your Grace,' said Mr Fraser.

'I was once a cellist, you know.' The Duchess made a movement with her hands, drawing a bow across her knees. 'My cello playing made the king weep. But now my fingers are old. It is only I who weep.'

'Well, at least you've made it to our beautiful school,' said Mr Fraser.

'This place *is* beautiful,' said Lady Anne, who had marched over to stand behind the Duchess's elbow. She pushed herself forward. 'It's like stumbling across a little hollow of perfection. It was my family's, not so long ago. All of it.' She threw back her arm, and took in everything, as if she wanted to pick up the valley and keep it for herself. Her gaze swept round the walls of the courtyard. Her eyes grazed the shrubs where Edward was hiding. He ducked, knowing she'd seen him. He could still hear their voices.

'Do you know, when I was small, and used to live here, there were many ghost stories about this place. I really do think that it is haunted. It really ought to be, don't you think?' Edward remembered the ice creature. He knew that there was something extraordinary going on, and a small bird of fear began fluttering in his chest. Lady Anne began to shift round towards where Edward was.

'Why do you think so?' The Duchess shifted her head to the side, questioning.

'The first night that I came here, I could have sworn that I saw a little boy – quite timid, and white, in a bush, of all places! But when I asked Alex here,' said Lady Anne, pointing to Fraser, 'he said there couldn't have been anyone. Can you imagine! I must have been dreaming. And over there, just now, I saw the most familiar face, peeping out.'

The fear in Edward began to spread throughout his body, and yet he had to stay to hear Lady Anne. She started subtly shepherding the little group towards where he crouched. 'Perhaps you can humour me, and we can check – otherwise I shall have terrible nightmares!'

'It shouldn't have been one of the boys,' said Fraser. 'It must have been a trick of the light.'

'Perhaps it was a dream person,' said the Duchess. 'Or maybe one of your ancestors, come to tell you of buried treasure! I know all about that sort of thing.'

'Perhaps it was,' said Lady Anne. 'I should be careful. There are things in this valley, trapped in the rustle of branches, in the cracks between books, which no one can understand.'

They were silent for a moment. Edward wished he were back in the safety of the dormitory, where he was real, not a figment of Lady Anne's imagination, a trick of the evening light and a cocktail glass.

'Hey,' said a voice. Edward jumped, thinking in horror it was Mrs Phipps. He turned round to face Mandy. 'What're you doing out here?'

'Ssh!' said Edward. This was definitely the real Mandy, her brown hair falling around her cheeks.

'Why are you so jumpy?'

'You'd be if you'd seen what I had . . .' He quickly explained what happened in the cold room. 'I don't know what it was, but I know it wanted . . . something from me. What did you find out?'

'That explains what I saw,' she said. 'Look, I haven't got much time. I saw those two witches in the staff room. Mrs Phipps . . . she's not *real*. She *evaporated*.'

Edward saw the group, led by Lady Anne, approaching the bushes and was suddenly seized with a violent spasm.

'What's the matter?' said Mandy.

'Nothing . . .' He pressed his fingers into his temples, trying to make the buzzing noise stop, but it wouldn't go away, and it was then that they heard a terrible shout. Fraser, the Duchess and Lady Anne all stopped, and looked around.

It was a sound that should not be heard at a cocktail party in the English countryside. It was a scream, long and painful. Edward didn't care now whether anyone saw him. Everyone was looking in the direction of the noise. Something was moving towards the party, something that was bubbling with rage.

It was Mr Bartlett. He was stumbling along, shouting incoherently, babbling a stream of rubbish, full of sound and fury. His tie was askew, hair at angles, he was clutching a bottle. He was splashing wine everywhere. He wandered up to the party, not noticing the commotion that he was causing. He was laughing.

Murmurs of worry were running through the crowd.

Edward watched Bartlett approaching, grateful that his appearance had deflected Lady Anne away from him.

'What is he doing?' asked Mandy.

The buzzing noise had risen to a shriek in Edward's head, and he was finding it difficult to balance. He held on to the wall for support, though it felt as if the force within him was so strong he could break down the Manor and bring all of its secrets crashing with it.

'Are you all right?' said Mandy. She was watching Edward, concerned, her attention diverted from the scene below. But Edward did not reply.

He saw that Imp had taken an interest in Mr Bartlett

and was sniffing and snuffling around his shiny brown brogues. He watched Bartlett swatting at the beast. 'Bloody irritating bloody little dog,' he said.

'Come on, Geoffrey. It's time we went home, friend. Come on.' Edward heard that O'Brien was speaking in the tone of voice he used when he spoke to Imp.

The dog was yapping and whimpering around Bartlett's legs. Bartlett was becoming increasingly annoyed. He swatted and Imp growled, showing his terrible teeth.

'Calm down, Geoffrey. Here, Imp. Come here. Imperative!' said O'Brien desperately.

Mr Bartlett wrenched free of O'Brien's grasping arm, and to Edward and Mandy's horror and disgust started to kick the dog, hard. Edward felt each kick as if it were aimed at his ribs, and doubled up, coughing. Mandy tried to comfort him, but he brushed her off.

'I have to watch this.'

Bartlett grabbed hold of Imp. A circle widened out around them. Edward saw Bartlett grappling with Imp. His hands were around Imp's throat. The dog was writhing, frantic; there was squealing and yipping and Mr O'Brien was shouting too and then, suddenly, there was nothing. Mr Bartlett held the dog aloft, triumphant, like a seer who has read the entrails and seen destruction, and Edward realised, along with Mandy

117

and the rest of the crowd, as the noise in his head rose to an unbearable pitch, he realised, with a sickening, final crunch in his stomach, that Imp was dead.

Edward saw the crowd of people widen around O'Brien, and saw O'Brien being sick on the grass, globules of spit sprayed from his mouth. The science master wiped the back of his hand across his lips and a long string of mucous joined his jaw and his hand, like a spider's silk.

It was as if someone had turned off a switch and sucked all the noise out of the party. People held their glasses halfway to their lips, unsure how to react. Edward noticed that only Lady Anne ate her olives, slowly and deliberately, holding a glass of sea-dark wine.

O'Brien held his hands to his eyes, bent over and vomited on to the grass again, heaving and shuddering. Mrs Ferrers ran to him, alarmed. Mr Bartlett let out a scream like a frenzied warrior. He tried to get to O'Brien, who stood, bent over, waving away any help, coughing up a stream of clear bile. He held Imp aloft, and ran into the centre of the courtyard, whooping and yelling, and, as if it were the climax of an ancient ritual, he placed the body of the dog Imp where the pillar had been. He turned round and yelled, as if he were expecting applause, or praise, or for them all to join in his exultation.

And then he started weeping. Edward and Mandy could not bear to watch him. It was bad enough when one of the boys cried. But Bartlett was in a position of authority, and he was now just a mass of wobbling phlegm and flesh. Then a change came over him; he stopped sobbing, and stood up, looking around at the world as if he had not noticed it before.

'Geoffrey?' said Fraser. 'Come with me.' Bartlett went with him like a foal, shaky and trusting. Noise slowly started seeping back into the party, and it soon rose to a roar, and as if in opposition, that in Edward's mind abated.

'What happened there?' said Mandy.

'I . . . I don't know,' said Edward. 'But listen to me. You've got to keep watching Phipps and Lady Anne. I don't know what they're up to. But they're dangerous. Listen to what they say to each other. You've got to help me. You can listen in on them when they're not paying attention. OK?'

Mandy nodded. Edward escaped back up to the dorms, his heart racing and his mouth dry. He leapt on to his bed. His dorm-mates turned to look at him, interested. 'You'd never believe,' he said. Then he stopped. They were all standing by the window. They had all heard the fracas below, but couldn't make out exactly what was going on. Their view was obscured by the shifting branches of a tree.

'What?' said someone.

'Nothing . . .' he said. Because he could feel under his pillow the presence of something and he put his hand under it to find the book. It had come back, externalised itself.

What he had seen when he'd opened the book came back to him. That impulse he had felt then for Mr Bartlett's destruction, for Imp's death, had somehow come true. That awful creature that he had seen in the book, that had asked him what he wanted before the knight had rescued him, had drawn it out of him and made it real.

Edward could hardly sleep. All that night he felt the presence of the book. It radiated a gloating, glutted complacence. All night he dreamt of destroying it, to stop its powers. But he did not think that he would be able to. Though somewhere, in the back of his mind, which he hardly dared to admit, he felt a grim sense of satisfaction at Mr Bartlett's humiliation.

Seven

wls made their eerie cries outside the dormitory window; Edward thought he heard the thundering of hooves in the courtyard, but when he looked out of the window there was nothing there. He looked at his watch in the moonlight – it was three o'clock in the morning. He hadn't been able to sleep. The book was sitting under his mattress. He felt a bending of reality, as if a weight had been pressed down upon a thin sheet of plastic. He had read about the invisible dark matter that makes up the universe, and he wondered if that was what the book was made of.

Impatient, weary, strained, he decided to take it out again. As quietly as he could, he got out of bed to reach under his mattress for the book, and leapt on to the window seat.

He gripped it firmly and, ignoring the pulse of pain

that throbbed up his arms, opened the book. The drawing of the man and the woman confronted him again. But this time he was prepared for the nightmarish results. The picture started to move. A great rushing noise filled his ears. He found himself speaking to the book, asking it for help. And, as if it were some great, wild intelligence, it seemed to answer him.

Something was different now. He felt detached from his body. Something was grabbing hold of him, and pulling him – his consciousness – out. With a creeping sense of horror he realised that he had somehow been yanked free, and for a second he saw his body lying on its back. How calm I look, he thought, terrified, and he was sucked into the blackness of the book.

He was falling, fast, and before he knew it he'd hit the ground, hard. He rolled over. Raising himself up on an elbow gingerly, he looked around. He was in a thicket. There was a low sun just visible through the trees, making little shards of beams. He felt the warm dampness of grass beneath him. A smell of late summer, the richness of fennel. He was dressed, incongruously, in his pyjamas. Slightly bruised from the fall, he got up, dusting off twigs and leaves.

'You are lucky, child,' said a voice, gentle, low, and Edward spun round to find himself staring at a knight.

'What do you want?' said Edward, on his guard. The

knight's helm was off. His sprightly horse was tethered nearby, munching on long grasses.

'Edward, do not fear me. There are many worse things than I. You must listen to me. There is great danger. I have chosen you as the one to aid me in fighting it. You are the carrier, Edward. It is a difficult task, and you have many enemies already.'

Me? thought Edward. You have chosen me? Confusion and fear spread through him, but he tried to stay strong. How was he to know that it wasn't another trick, like the ice monster?

'How do I know that I can trust you?' he said, as forcefully as he could.

The knight looked solemn. 'You must trust me, child. You have a task, and it must be performed, or else your world will be overcome by those who seek what you have.'

Edward was still not sure what to think. The knight noticed his discomfort. He unsheathed his sword, the metallic noise sounding loud in the quiet of the forest. Edward stepped back.

'Wait, child.' The knight knelt down. 'Here.' He held out the sword to Edward, its pommel towards the boy. 'Take it.' The knight's neck was bare.

Edward held the sword above the knight's head. The low sun was warm, he heard the horse snorting, whinnying to itself. He had never held a sword before. It was heavy. For a moment he wondered what it would be like just to draw back the blade and let it fall on to the knight's neck. He shifted his weight, considering how much strength it would take to make a clean break. Would he be able to hack through in one go? The thought made him shudder and he lowered the sword.

'It's OK,' he said. 'Please, get up.'

Slowly, assuredly, the knight raised himself. Edward held out the brand to him. 'Thank you,' he said. Sunlight flashed off the knight's armour.

'Where are we?' said Edward.

'In a world created for you by the book – the Other Book. When you first opened it, you lost yourself to its dark power and allowed another to control you. This time you have shown you can control it. You are not strong enough to use its full powers.

'Too long has the Book been absent, too long have I fought against the creatures of the Other World. I am weakening and it is time for the prophecy to be fulfilled. You must restore the Other Book. You have seen what it can do. And I must tell you, when you use it next, if you do not put up defences then she will hear you and manipulate you again. At all costs you must keep it from her.' The knight's face was set, stern.

'Defences? What do you mean?'

'Strengthen your mind.'

'But how . . . how will I be able to do that?'

'Just think of what you love most. Think of your family, your friends, those people with whom you feel strong.' The knight looked sad for a moment. 'At the due time, you will also have to make a sacrifice.'

'What? What sort of sacrifice?' Edward felt a sense of purpose fill him. He looked at the knight's kind, handsome face. It seemed to Edward that this was the moment he had been looking for, all of his life. He wanted to do what the knight asked of him. It was a quest, something in which he could prove himself. 'I'll do whatever it takes,' he said quietly.

The knight nodded. 'Excellent, child,' he said. 'Now it is meet that I instruct you –' He stopped. 'Hold fast!'

The sun was dimming. Where before it had been a pleasant, orange glow, it was fading; before Edward's eyes it began to descend, rapidly. The onset of cold was sudden; Edward shivered in his thin pyjamas.

'She hears us!' The knight drew his sword. 'Be wary! Lord knows what she has sent . . .'

The forest was becoming darker. Edward watched the bright green leaves of the welcoming trees begin to wither and fall off, shrivelling up until the warm bark turned black. The grass too browned as if it had been scorched.

He sensed that many creatures were concealed around him, their eyes all bent on him, and Edward had a dizzying impression of standing on the edge of a vast, howling abyss, buffetted by strong winds.

The knight shouted at him, 'You must go. Now! *Beware those who seek it for their own gain . . . the line of the wizard and witch is strong . . .*' The knight's horse whinnied in fear, and he went to it. 'Calm, Beaumont,' he said. He hoisted himself up on it.

Creatures began to come out of the woods, creatures that Edward had seen when he had opened the Book for the first time. 'Go! Go now!'

'How?' shouted Edward.

'Think yourself back into your body!' The knight settled himself into the saddle. Bloodthirsty and lordly he looked, his blade shining as he swirled it around his head.

'I don't understand! I don't understand!' said Edward helplessly; as the creatures began to snake out of the trees, he thought as hard as he could of his bed and his body: he felt himself swirling, whirling, he felt the force of a terrible wind; there was a shattering noise.

He was breathless, choking. Shivering. He did not dare to open his eyes. Slowly, blinking, he crumpled them open.

126

He was safe. He was on the window seat. He fell into bed, ashen-faced.

The Other Book . . . that was what it was called. So strange, and terrible, and it was his. He put it back under his mattress, not daring to keep it near his skin, and drifted into fitful, dream-haunted sleep.

Eight

he next day when the bell for assembly rang, everyone was in a sombre mood. Masters rushed here and there, hurried and harassed, answering questions sharply. There was absolutely no question of a cover-up. All the boys with dorms that faced on to the courtyard had heard the disturbance. Some had seen what had happened. It was fast becoming a myth. Bartlett the Puppy Slayer.

The walls of Great Hall were lined with masters. They were all grave, in various pensive poses. The boys were all murmuring quietly as they lined up, which was odd, because usually they would be running around, playing games, until they were quietened down by the master in charge. Will came up to Edward.

'Nice bags,' he said.

'Huh?'

'Under your eyes.'

'Oh yeah. I couldn't sleep last night.' He didn't want to say anything else, and Will didn't push him.

Edward wasn't really paying attention to what was going on. He thought about the raven, the prophecy, Mr Bartlett and the knight, and how they were connected. He wondered whether the raven had been a sign, who had written the prophecy. The knight had said, 'You have seen what it can do.' Could it be possible that he, through the Other Book, had caused Bartlett's breakdown? And the awesomeness of the task which had been set him: restore the Other Book . . . but to whom?

Fraser was looking strained. 'Sit down,' he said, very quietly, but everyone heard him. Fraser glanced gloomily around the room. 'Last night you may have heard, or seen, many things. I'd like to set the matter straight. Mr Bartlett has been taken ill. He has gone on an extended sabbatical and we hope that he will return when he is better.'

This blatant lie caused murmurings from the boys. They all knew that Mr Bartlett had done something horrific.

'Silence,' said Fraser, and there was silence for a moment, but then the huge doors of Great Hall opened. Everybody swivelled to look at the latecomer.

Lady Anne de la Zouche shimmered in, followed by Mrs Phipps. Lady Anne settled into a chair by the door, but Phipps remained standing. She began to shuffle, slowly, around the back of the room, her malign gaze grazing over every head in the room. Edward's skin was crawling. She had stopped, deliberately, at the end of his row. He could feel her looking at him. It felt as if she could see deep into his brain, into its coiling, gleaming folds, and tear out the thoughts. Edward tried to make his mind blank, and focused on the comforting figure of Mr Fraser, though all he could think about was the Other Book. It hadn't disappeared. He had locked it into his overnight case, and stashed it under some papers and boxes under his bed. He hoped it was safe there. The knight had said he could now control it. Maybe it only disappeared when it needed to make his thoughts real.

'I have another announcement to make. We're very lucky – we won't have to look far for a replacement English teacher. One of our governors has kindly agreed to step in. Lady Anne de la Zouche,' said Mr Fraser, and motioned to her to come up. She walked slowly, elegantly, up the middle of Great Hall. Edward stopped breathing, and elbowed Will in the gut.

She walked like a model up a catwalk – poised, confident. When she stopped by Mr Fraser, he looked wan and tired by comparison with her brightness.

The headmaster shook her warmly by the hand. 'Lady Anne was at Magdalen with me. She read English literature.' He glanced at her, and she nodded warmly. 'Lady Anne is intimately connected to the school. Her family, the de la Zouches, were the owners of Oldstone Manor until the 1970s. It is an old, old title – and the only one that passes directly through the female line as well as the male. There are many de la Zouche tombstones in the churchyard, and indeed many portraits dotted around Oldstone. There are two or three in here.' He pointed to the enormous portrait of the vicious-looking man above the huge fireplace.

Edward remembered that the tombstone he had put the raven on had been a de la Zouche grave . . . maybe that had something to do with Lady Anne. Was it possible that she could control people? Who was it that had made Imp leave the raven? Edward shuddered, imagining her as a mad puppet-master, swinging little figures from her hands.

'Lady Anne will continue to stay in the guest house, which is, as you all know, *strictly* out of bounds. Now, boys. Let's all give Lady Anne a Rousing School Welcome!'

This was the cue for the boys to clap and stamp their feet, which they did, very loudly. At Mr Fraser's signal

131

they gave three cheers. Edward thought that they were all deeply affected by Lady Anne. It was as if a magnet had been put down on a sheet of paper scattered with iron filings that grouped around it. He wondered if anyone would be able to resist her.

Lady Anne made a small gesture with her hand, and the school was silent.

'Good morning, boys,' she said. 'I would like to say that I have been looking forward to returning here for many years, since my family left when I was a young girl. This place is extremely special to me. I am only sad that it is someone else's misfortune that has given me the opportunity to throw myself fully into the life of Oldstone Manor. I hope that you will all help me to settle into the school as seamlessly as possible.

'I have a special announcement for Eudoky. Instead of your usual English lesson this morning, I would like to meet you all individually so that we can get to know each other and plan the exciting things we shall be doing for your scholarships. So if you could all wait in the form room,' she continued, 'I will come to collect you at intervals. Thank you very much.' She smiled the smile of a goddess, and melted to the side of the room. Mr Fraser took the floor again, and launched the assembly into 'Onward Christian So-o-o-oldiers', which the music mistress, voluptuous Mrs Frank, seemed to bang out rather faster than normal.

The boys all sang a little more loudly and brashly than usual, because they were showing off to Lady Anne. Assembly finished with a burst of school pride, Bartlett's shame dispersed. The boys went straight out to their first lessons, which would start in a couple of minutes.

'Hey, Strangore,' said Edward as they filed into Eudoky. 'I'll talk to you at break, OK?' He was nervous, excited, ideas flashing around his mind. Will nodded. Edward didn't want to tell his cousin, but he had a plan. If he really was 'chosen' as the knight had told him, then would Will have the same experience as he did? He would have to find out.

Double Latin was seriously hard work that day. Everybody's head was down, nibs scratched against exercise books, there was much consulting of grammar books and dictionaries, and before Edward knew it the bell rang for break, and as everyone else left Eudoky, he grabbed Will on his way out.

'Strangore,' he said, fiercely, tugging his elbow. Will peered at Edward as if he were a long way away. 'I said I needed to talk to you.' He realised quite how odd he sounded, gulped, and tried to calm himself.

'OK. Let's go. But be quick about it. I haven't finished my maths prep. I don't want to risk a kak. I'm in with a chance of winning this week.' Strangore always took the competitions far too seriously.

They sneaked into the deserted dorms. No one was in the courtyard below, where the disrupted party had been. The whole place had been cleared by the efficient cleaning staff, and not a crumb, not a plastic plate, not a dropped strawberry remained. Edward took Will to the window seat.

Edward reached under his bed and unlocked his case. He took out the Other Book. It seemed to him as if it were alive. He shuddered as he picked it up. The pain was less sharp than it had been before, though, and it did not make him bleed. He laid it reverently on the bed.

'It's certainly real,' said Will, suitably impressed, feeling the waves of power coming off it. He reached out a finger to touch it, and recoiled as if he'd been stung by a scorpion. A small drop of blood formed at the tip of his finger. 'Ow! God, it's really true!'

Sitting down on the window seat, they decided that Will would open the Other Book just as Edward had.

'So what do I do?' Will scratched his chin.

'You just have to . . . open it.' But Edward, in his excitement, had forgotten to tell him about putting up defences. And someone felt the power surge, someone felt their blood sing, and sent something out towards the source of it.

'Here goes.' Will took the Book and opened it. Watching him, Edward saw him cringe with pain.

'Keep holding,' he said. Edward watched Will stiffen, his eyes misting over. He waved a hand in front of him but Will did not register anything. He sat still, like a carved monument, eyes blank, face cold.

'Will?' said Edward. Will did not reply. Edward sat down on the bed and waited.

There was a trembling, so faint that Edward could hardly feel it at first. He wondered if it was coming from his own body. It happened again, much stronger this time. The room was definitely shaking.

Edward went to Will and shook him. Will was blacked-out, as if he'd been concussed. The room shook again. 'Come on, Will, wake up,' said Edward.

Hissing noises started at the edges of sound. The wallpaper, blue and white stripes, began to shiver, and then, to Edward's amazement, patterns drawn on the paper began to unravel, and to snake out towards Will and Edward. The dimensions of the room changed. Walls bent in, curved.

Lines were drawing across Will, and he was becoming tangled in a net. A throbbing noise filled the room. Edward tried to reach him but he too was caught. Around his feet little loops had been drawn, and he could not move. Some horrific spider was drawing its web across them.

The loops were tightening around Will's arms and neck now. Edward tore at them, but every time he broke one they came together again.

'Will! Come on! Try and break free!' But Will did not answer.

More and more of the living lines were enveloping them. And Edward could do nothing. The Other Book was with Will. He could not even hope to control it. How could he have let this happen?

Nine

dward clawed at his bindings. The door began to open, and a figure came in, humanoid in shape. It advanced towards them. *Caught*, it whispered, and Edward felt all the hope go out of him. He thought of the knight. Help me, he thought. Please, I can't fail you now . . .

There was a flash of light, a terrible tearing sound, and somebody, bright and noble, stood in between Edward and the figure. The lines, which had now become as thick as ropes, shrivelled away quickly into nothingness. The figure let out a shriek of disappointment, and vanished.

Though the light burned only for a second, even when Edward screwed up his eyes he could still feel it. When the light disappeared, he slowly opened his eyes again and saw strange colours in the air. It was the knight, thought Edward. He looked around.

The room was as it had been.

Will came to, and Edward felt a sudden surge of painful energy. He knew the Other Book had leapt back into him.

'Will! What happened to you?'

'Well . . .' Will was reticent. A battle was going on inside him.

'Did you see anything?'

'No,' said Will. He was a scientist. What he had seen defied rational explanation. Therefore, as far as he could work out, it had not happened. If he denied it, then it would not exist. It was as simple as that.

'Are you sure?' asked Edward, troubled. He could see how pale and trembling Will was, and remembered how ill he had felt after being sucked into the Book for the first time.

'Right,' said Strangore. He got up with difficulty. 'Now that we've got that over with, let's go down to Eudoky. We're late already. And we're meeting Lady Anne. So you can ask her about any conspiracy that she happens to be plotting. All right?'

Edward did not push him any further.

They made their way down to Eudoky, not speaking. Edward had expected his cousin to have the same experience as him. But he clearly hadn't. Unless

Strangore was lying. But why would he? Edward could not guess that Will was troubled, deeply. His ordered world had been invaded, his concrete beliefs had been liquified, and his response was to deny. Edward thought that if the same thing had happened to Will as had happened to him, then he would have to be on the alert for Will behaving strangely, and then he would know. He would know if the Book caused these things. He would know if he was not going mad. And he would also know if the Book had been chosen for him. It had come back to him after Will had read it. If it goes to Will after it does whatever Will's made it do, then I'll know, he thought.

They slipped quietly into Eudoky through the back door. Everyone was at their desks, reading Tennyson.

Edward and Will took their places in silence. Edward took out his book, looking over at his cousin for some sign of camaraderie or complicity, but Will was bent over the poem. Edward returned to his musings, which were troubled by the knight's words, and the ever-present, low-level noise of the Book. It was like having a radio station play white noise all the time.

He couldn't concentrate on the words of *Idylls of the King*, and instead found an interesting object of contemplation in a picture on the wall – *The Lady of Shalott* by John William Waterhouse. A woman, dressed in a white dress, sat in a boat covered in rich tapestries, three candles guttering in the breeze. Her face was set in eternal sadness, the animals and woods around her indifferent. She was dying, and nobody cared.

So he didn't notice when Montgomery, the boy before him, had come in, and was standing by his desk all but shouting, 'You're up next, Pollock.'

Reluctantly, almost stickily, Edward went through into the corridor, leaving his paperback face down on his desk. Lady Anne had got someone to set up a table and two chairs, and was sitting in one of them. She had a pile of folders and a gold pen, with which she was making notes on a pad of lined A4 paper. He didn't admit it to himself, but he was terrified. He knew that Lady Anne had something to do with the ice monster and the attack in the dormitory on him and Will. He was on the alert.

'Edward Pollock. How nice to finally meet you, *properly*, as it were. Do sit down.' She shuffled the papers, and searched through them. 'Ah, here you are.' She pulled out a file which had Edward's name on it in thick, black letters. She took out the first piece of paper.

'Edward Scipio Aubrey Pollock. What interesting middle names.' Lady Anne flipped her pen around on her finger.

Edward said nothing.

'Now . . . I've been wondering why you look so familiar. Do you think we have met before?'

Edward shook his head. 'No, Lady Anne.'

'Are you sure? Because you do look so familiar.' She flipped her pen again, and studied the report. 'Ah, yes. It says here . . .' she shuffled the papers, 'that you're quite the reader.'

'Not really,' said Edward, trying to sound offhand.

'Now, Mr Pollock! Mr Fraser tells me that you're always in the library. A lot of those books were there when my family was here, you know.' She leant back in her chair, and put down her papers. She placed her long, thin fingers on her knees.

'There must be quite a few treasures in there. Have you ever found anything in there? Anything that's really beautiful, or really old, or so marvellous that you weren't able to put it down?'

Her eyes rested on Edward's. They were green and calm, oases in the sudden desert of her face. Edward felt drowsy, contented.

'You know, Edward,' she said, leaning in confidentially, 'I've studied a lot of books over the years. I think that this library of ours must have some real gems in it. Don't you?'

'I do,' said Edward warmly.

'Real gems, Edward. Books which leave your spine aching from sitting up all night reading them; books whose characters live in the bright corners of your mind. Books which hold the limits of space and time within them; books which teach you all that man knows and all that man wants. Books, Edward, are *power*. And once you learn how to control this power – Edward – the possibilities are endless.' She was speaking quietly but with such a deadly edge that Edward was frightened. Something of her hunger showed itself in her eyes now, and the strength of it caused Edward to stand up very quickly.

'I think it's time for the next boy, Lady Anne,' said Edward and, getting up, prepared to rush through the door.

'Why, don't be silly,' he heard her say. 'Come back here.'

The cold iron in her voice made Edward turn round.

'Sit down.'

He sat.

'Edward. I won't play around any more. I saw you on the drive the first night I arrived here.'

'So what?' said Edward.

'Will you help me, Edward?' she said.

'Help you to do what?'

'To settle into the school. That's all I want, Edward.

To be a good teacher, until a replacement comes, and then to go back to being a governor. And to see the house that belonged to my family in good hands.'

Edward shrugged.

'So,' she said. 'Are you on my side? We can do so many great things together.'

Her words hung in the air like fireworks, blazing against the sky, promising glorious things, and Edward was tempted by the noise, the light, the wonder; but the sad face of the knight came back to him, and he said, 'I'll think about it.'

'You're making a very serious mistake, Edward,' said Lady Anne. She could feel the pulse of the Book within him; it had called to her all her life, and now that it was so near her and she could not get it, she could hardly bear it.

Edward found that his throat was constricting. He noticed Lady Anne was holding a rubber, and that she was squeezing it. He coughed out, 'Stop it.'

But she pressed harder, and he felt the weight crushing his throat. Just when he thought he was about to pass out, she released the rubber. Edward sprang out of his chair.

'Well,' she said, 'when you have thought about it, you know where to find me. Thank you, Edward. Call in the next boy. Rolandson.'

Edward went out. He sat down at his desk, calling the next boy on the way. He was hugely grateful that his next lesson was Greek and that safe, normal, sensible Mr Fraser was coming. But he realised that in Mr Fraser lay no avenue of escape from the burden that he carried; in Mr Fraser was no hope of rescue. And to make it worse, Strangore still wouldn't look at him.

Why shouldn't I help her? he thought. How do I know that she wants to be bad? How do I know *anything*? He felt his neck with trepidation. He wondered if there were marks round it. It was no use. How could he fight against this person? He did not understand her, or her powers. Why shouldn't I give it to Lady Anne and get rid of it? It would only take a minute . . . and with this note of despair, like the sound of a horn at the death of a hound, he slumped on to the scarred wood of his desk.

Ten

he lesson went on. The rest of the boys filed in to see Lady Anne. Edward watched the sun filling the valley with its rays, so thick it was like mist. Eudoky had a stone floor, which kept the classroom cool in summer, but Edward felt far from cool. The last boy came into the room. Lady Anne did not follow him.

The ancient piano in the corner creaked and grunted lazily. There was a tapping at the window, startling the boys into action. They all looked up, surprised to see Lady Anne outside, wreathed in smiles, with flowers woven into her hair, wearing a long blue dress.

'Well, come on, then!' she said. 'Don't stand there gawping like a lot of fish! Come with me!' She started walking off in the direction of the pond and the river. The boys all stared at each other and then got up, rushing out of the room. In other circumstances, Edward would have welcomed this, would have felt like a young cavalier going a-maying with his Queen in the greenwood. But suspicion had settled in his heart.

Lady Anne led them down to the pond, where the large oak tree stood. She walked around it with a grace and beauty that made them all quiet – except Edward, who was on edge. She embraced the tree for a second, then smiled.

'Sit down boys!' she said. 'I'm going to read you the tale of Merlin and Vivien from *Idylls of the King*.'

The trees were trailing their branches in the water like schoolboys in a boat, holding their hands in the river as they drift downstream. Sunlight splintered off the water. The boys arranged themselves around Lady Anne, who was sitting right underneath the tree. Edward lay on his front and buried his face in the grass. Lady Anne started to read:

'*A storm was coming, but the winds were still,*
And in the wild woods of Broceliande,
Before an oak, so hollow huge and old
It look'd a tower of ruin'd mason work,
At Merlin's feet the wily Vivien lay.'

She read quietly, with a gentle expression that made the

scenes come vividly to life. Edward couldn't help but think that Lady Anne had chosen the story of Merlin and Vivien for a reason.

He remembered the prophecy – *the line of the wizard and the witch is strong*. What did it mean? And the Ms and Vs around the tomb? In the hazy summer heat of the day, with the calm voice of Lady Anne washing over them, Edward lay, holding his nervousness in secret. The boys were around her, squires enchanted at the feet of Vivien herself.

Lady Anne was reaching the middle of the poem.

> '*A little glassy-headed hairless man,*
> *Who lived alone in a great wild on grass;*
> *Read but one book . . .*'

A book, he thought. But one book. How strange to read only one book.

> '*. . . to him the wall*
> *That sunders ghosts and shadow-casting men*
> *Became a crystal, and he saw them thro' it . . .*'

The wall between ghosts and men? Edward cast back to the prophecy . . . something about the wall between ghosts and men . . . He couldn't remember. Lady

Anne's voice was so soothing, he couldn't think very clearly. The Other Book was beginning to stir and buzz, as it had on the night of the party.

But Edward was almost transported into the poem. Lady Anne read beautifully, evocatively, and the warm sun, the delicious smell of the grass, the gentle lapping of the pond and the whispering of the trees all combined to make him drowsy and forgetful. He pressed his mouth against the grass and felt the world spin around him. He was drifting away.

> '. . . and his book came down to me.
> And Vivien answer'd smiling saucily:
> "Ye have the book: the charm is written in it."'

Edward rolled over, sitting up, his legs out straight in front of him, a clump of torn grass in his hand, a crushed daisy staining his fingers with its yellowness. Noisy rumblings and a clatter of glass equipment could be heard approaching. Lady Anne read the words again. This was a trap. She was hoping to see Edward's reaction, hoping to quell him into admitting what he knew. She was taking a chance, but it was built on strong grounds. Her agent had already been unsuccessful. Now it was up to her.

'Ye have the book: the charm is written in it.'

Her gaze was directed at Edward. The Other Book was humming, mounting infinitely slowly, obscuring his thought processes. The science class was getting nearer, led by Mr O'Brien, bent on some pond-dipping expedition. Everyone turned their heads to look. Lady Anne had lost the attention of her audience. She put her book down, but remained seated on the grass, her legs stretched out sideways, long and elegant.

'Ye have the book!' she said quietly, in Edward's direction. There was no mistaking it. She had fixed Edward with the eyes of a cobra and he could feel the sudden thinning between worlds that signalled the workings of the Other Book, the jostling of hideous creatures.

Edward watched Mr O'Brien march up to them. A group of chattering boys, all carrying test tubes, nets and other things from the lab followed him. They set up a few yards away from where Edward was sitting. Lady Anne picked up the book and continued to read. Her words were now interrupted by splashes and shrieks from Mr O'Brien's class. Edward could hear fragments of O'Brien's commands, but he was intent on listening to Lady Anne.

'Naked ignorance delivers brawling judgments . . .'

She said these last words with particular emphasis. Edward looked at Will. But nothing was happening to him. Instead he felt the same buzzing he had felt before Bartlett had killed Imp . . . he prepared himself for the worst.

Lane Glover was splashing around, knocking into people, putting pondweed on to their heads. Lady Anne stopped reading and looked across. Edward could see that she was immensely annoyed. When she rearranged her legs, to Edward she looked coiled up, like a snake.

Eudoky was now more interested in Lane Glover's antics than in Lady Anne's reading, though Edward just caught her last words, which she read out as loudly as she could manage without shouting:

'And every square of text an awful charm,
Writ in a language that has long gone by . . .'

Every square of text an awful charm, in a language long gone by. Edward was suddenly cold.

Guy Lane Glover had just knocked over a glass tube arrangement. Mr O'Brien was shouting at him. Lady Anne, without saying anything, got up and walked away to get Mr Fraser. She smiled to herself. Everything was playing into her hands. Eudoky didn't notice. All eyes were on O'Brien.

'Lane Glover! What the heck do you think you're doing! Stop it at once!'

'Nothing, sir, wasn't me, sir, didn't do it, sir!' said Lane Glover. He ran back to where he'd been thrusting pondweed down Peake's shirt.

'Glover! Stop it! Or you're going straight to the headmaster!'

Edward found that he could not pay very much attention to the scene in front of him; the noise and whirl of the Other Book was too much for him, and it was all he could do not to black out. His face was outwardly calm, but his hands were gripping the grass so tightly that his knuckles were standing out white like the snowy peaks of mountains. This is it, he thought. This must be what Will felt when he opened the Book. Edward glanced across towards him. Will looked disturbed.

There was a sudden silence from the boys. Edward heard O'Brien saying 'like your father' and then Guy saying, very quietly, 'What did you say, sir?' In the pause after this, Edward felt the future waiting for him like an arrow about to be loosed. He felt a pattern forming, he sensed pieces slotting into place, when Guy hurled himself at O'Brien and started beating him with his fists, yelling and screaming.

O'Brien started shouting too, but Lane Glover was

strong and quick. The science master was trying to grab his wrists, and they grappled. Someone shoved, they scrabbled, and then Lane Glover sprawled backwards, crashing through test tubes, straight into the pond, bringing O'Brien swearing after him.

Edward saw Lady Anne turn the corner with Mr Fraser.

O'Brien and Lane Glover were splashing around in the pond, covered in weeds, spluttering. Lane Glover was still fighting, jumping at O'Brien, trying to drench him even more. Mr Fraser came to the edge of the pond, and looked down, arms folded, an inscrutable expression on his face. O'Brien said nothing. Lane Glover might have been in tears, but it was hard to tell.

The Other Book relaxed its hold, and Edward released the grass. He saw that Will had fallen on his back, and wondered if he should go to him.

Then to his horror he found that the Book had metamorphosed, and he was holding the clammy thing in his hands. *It's come back to me*, thought Edward.

It was a clear sign. It was his. It had not chosen Will. He was not going mad. He had a task to fulfil.

'Well, you do look a sight, don't you,' said Mr Fraser, grimly, to O'Brien and Lane Glover. He turned to Lady Anne. 'Lady Anne, would you take all the boys up to the form rooms, and keep them there until I get back?' She nodded, with a slight moue of disappointment, because she could feel the sudden corporeal presence of the Other Book. The boys all trooped after her, collecting experiments and books hastily together. Edward lagged behind to see if he could run off and hide the Book, but Mr Fraser said, 'Go along now, Pollock,' then marched off with O'Brien and Glover.

Will was wandering just ahead. Edward grabbed him, quite roughly. Will tore away. Lady Anne was near them. She had felt the twisting of reality, the drawing together of strands of fates, and she was closing in on her prey.

'Get it away from me,' Will snarled. 'That thing . . . it's done something to me . . . it made me do something . . . I didn't want it to happen . . . something was pushing me . . . this creature, all hooded and odd, it forced me . . .'

Edward remembered the thing that had appeared when he'd first read the Book.

'*We can't let her get it*,' whispered Edward. 'You have to help me.'

Lady Anne sensed Will as the source of the turbulence. She headed towards him, slowly, moving through the boys with dreadful purpose, her regal fingers quivering slightly. Edward could see her eyes fixed on Will. They reached the form rooms.

She's made a mistake, thought Edward. *She thinks it's with Will.* He bent towards Will's ear. 'Pretend you've got it. I'll find the knight, get him to explain.' He remembered calling out to the knight, and the bright figure who had rescued them from the ropes in the dorm.

'What do you want me to do?' Will was crumpled.

'Create a diversion,' said Edward. He felt like a butterfly scrabbling at a windowpane, seeing freedom ahead of him but not knowing how to get there.

'What sort of diversion?'

'Too late,' said Edward, as Lady Anne came into the room, and Mrs Phipps appeared at the other door to the classroom. She radiated malevolence, occasionally making insect-like hissing noises, and they both advanced upon the boys. Edward gripped Will's arm. 'Sorry,' he said, and then he turned to Lady Anne. There was only one thing he could do.

'*It's with him,*' he said and, as they turned their attention to Will and bore down upon the shivering boy, he darted out of the room and ran for it. Those two seconds during which Lady Anne and Mrs Phipps seized Strangore, pretending to be concerned for his health, and realised that he was not carrying the Book at all, were enough for Edward to escape.

He sprinted out of the form rooms, round the corner and up a narrow gravel path which led to the woods. Clumps of hawthorn in bloom lined the path. Coming round a corner, he nearly slipped, but righted himself and carried on, beginning to pant in a ragged way. Come on, he said to himself. Temple. I'll make it to Temple.

His camp was in the north-west corner of the woods, hidden away near the boundaries of the school. Beyond it was totally out of bounds, fenced off by barbed wire. He came to the end of the path and powered on into the woods, darting around trees whose green, calm leaves made a silent, living cathedral. He was lucky that he knew every inch of the woods, or he might have fallen many times; he leapt over logs, dodged round stumps and once cleared a small ditch.

Even as he ran he saw himself laying the Other Book before Lady Anne, receiving her favour, becoming her equal. It was hot and he was sweating, the sunlight oppressive.

'Ye have the book,' she had said, staring right at him, through him, until he felt as if she was X-raying his mind and knew every little thought and impulse. He stumbled over a log, scrabbling for balance, twigs catching at his clothes.

He made it to Temple, pushing through the branches. The entrance was small and hidden. As he went in, the light filtering through the leaves made it seem as if he were underwater. He held his breath and heard the blood pounding in his ears. He looked around. It hadn't changed. Then he saw that someone had tied a small mirror to a branch. It felt uncomfortably like an eye fixed upon him, so he turned it round. He settled down and held the Other Book as if it were a lizard, slippery and alive.

He opened it and felt as if he was teetering on the edge of a precipice. From where she was standing in front of the Manor, Lady Anne felt the surge of power. 'Find him, Phipps,' she whispered to her henchwoman.

The signs were spiralling, burning in Edward's mind. He tensed himself, putting up barriers, thinking of what he loved the most. He felt strong. He fell headlong and came out into the green and gold of the dreamworld which the Other Book created for him.

The knight was sitting on a log, looking patient and tired.

'Who are you?' said Edward, before the knight could say anything.

'My name is Tristram de la Zouche.'

'Are you Lady Anne de la Zouche's ancestor?'

'I am. It was my tomb on which you laid the raven. It was a test, to prove your worth. The raven is the noble crest of the de la Zouches. You saw it given dignity. You showed you despised cruelty and would aid those in distress. I knew you were the right child. I knew you were pure, when I saw you converse with the spirits.'

A pure one will find it, thought Edward.

'I put *Idylls of the King* in the library as a guide for you, I showed you the Other Book.' Tristram came closer to Edward. 'The Other Book was our family's heirloom, the source of our power. Our honour – and our burden. The line continued here unbroken, since it began with Merlin and Vivien, for generations.' He stood up, and began to pace, fiddling with his scabbard.

The Ms and Vs on the tomb, thought Edward, and in the front of the Book. Merlin and Vivien. *The line of the wizard and witch* – it must be them.

'One of my ancestors was a foolish man. His name was Wentlake.' When Tristram said the name, his voice wavered slightly. 'He damned the old stories, and turned Oldstone into a haven for gamblers, drunkards and worse. He used the Other Book for great evil. It came to Merlin's notice. He sent guardians to Wentlake to try to persuade him to abandon his ways. But he slew them. Merlin sent more powerful agents, and they won, but at the price of Wentlake's life.

'The Other Book was poisoned. Wentlake's corrruption was of such great potency that the Book could not be restored until it had been purifed. And Wentlake's

157

son was destined to see that happen.' Tristram looked up, his eyes suffused with something Edward could not quite place – was it grief? Or pleasure?

He asked gently, 'What happened next?'

'Now the seed of evil is flourishing. Now you must see that the Other Book is returned to its rightful owner.'

'But who is it? Will you help me?'

A change came over Tristram. He was alert, his face strained, his body tensed. 'Something is approaching,' he said. 'Your body lies vulnerable. You must go.'

Edward imagined his body and experienced the fearful dislocating sense; then he was back in Temple, and he could hear someone coming though the woods. The Other Book was in his hands. It began to glow with sharp light. And it began to melt, and he felt it seeping into him like hot wax.

Temple was circular, and roofed by a low screen of branches. There was no other way for him to get out. He was enclosed. He could smell alcohol and he felt sick. The Other Book shone brilliantly for a second, and then there was nothing.

Edward could just make out a black, hulking shape. A hand grabbed him by the scruff of his neck. He held his breath. The smell of sweat was overpowering. Edward trembled. Something came into the centre of the round camp.

Eleven

he thing stank. Edward felt like retching but forced himself not to. It came into a patch of light.

Edward saw at once that it was Mr Bartlett.

Bartlett didn't have a beard – that must have been what he was using the mirror for. And he was still wearing the scratchy tweed suit which Edward detested so much. It was covered in dirt and was torn in several places. His shirt was untucked, and his tie, usually of such military precision, was undone. His shoes still shone, though they were beginning to look scuffed. Edward was so angry with him. Bartlett had violated Temple.

'It would be you, Pollock, wouldn't it?' Bartlett was shivering with fever, and his eyes shone. Edward felt as Imp must have felt before Mr Bartlett had killed him.

'Sit down, Pollock. Do. Sit down in my castle. An

Englishman's home and all that.' He laughed. 'It was a conspiracy, you know. A full-blown, gunpowder treason and whatsit conspiracy.'

Edward cleared his throat. 'What for, sir?'

'What for? What for? What do you think for? Imbecile.' He coughed and spat out a huge glob of phlegm. 'Do you think old Bartlett would be living here by choice? Of course not. It was a conspiracy to drive *me* out of Oldstone Manor.' He stopped talking, and scratched himself under his armpits. His hands fumbled in his pockets and he drew out a half-empty packet of tobacco. With trembling movements he rolled a cigarette and then, after many attempts, struck a match and lit it. Bartlett jabbed in the air with his roll-up. He coughed again, a wrenching cough that shook his frame. 'Bartlett's been hounded out – hah! Hounded out like the shivering *cur* he is.'

In that moment, Edward realised what the Book had done to him. And he felt a sort of pity for this man. His anger faded.

Edward heard branches crack. Bartlett spun round. 'Who's there?' he said.

A figure appeared, bent. It was Mrs Phipps. Edward felt fear expand in his body. Mrs Phipps leant forward and a voice issued from her mouth: 'You're wanted, Pollock. She is waiting.'

Edward could not push past her. The camp he had so lovingly built had become a prison.

And then he remembered. He remembered the spirits of the wood that he had seen in this very place. He focused his mind, and spoke to them. There was silence for a second, and then he heard creakings and rustlings.

He wondered whether what he was seeing was real – the branches of the trees were reaching around Mrs Phipps. He blinked, but when he looked again, they were twining round her arms, preventing her from moving. Ivy trailed across the ground and snaked around her ankles, pulling her aside. Logs piled up around her. Edward did not stop to wait, but ran. He heard Mr Bartlett saying, 'What the devil?' He looked behind him and saw Mrs Phipps struggling to break free from a thicket that had sprung up around her.

Now his only thought was to run. He didn't know where. The woods around him seemed to make way for him as he pelted along. When he came down the gravel path, he hesitated. The only thought in his mind was to take it to the highest authority around, and that was Mr Fraser. His mind set, he jumped down the three steps on to the drive, and careered towards the Manor.

He was halfway down it when Lady Anne came round the bend.

Keep going, he thought to himself. Keep going. Just go straight past her. He focused his gaze ahead of him and galloped ahead, passing her in a flash.

'Edward! Edward Pollock! I need to talk to you!' she called after him.

He'd made it down the drive. The friendly bulk of Oldstone Manor appeared ahead. He looked behind him.

There was the approaching figure of Mrs Phipps, shedding twigs and leaves. They were closing in on him. Edward ducked into the side door of the Manor and took a left turn down the passageway. He heard the heavy, oak front door squeaking open and dashed through a door opposite him. It led into a corridor which led straight into Kakophagy. He closed the door behind him and ran into the empty room – the tables had been cleared after supper and the kitchens were silent. He didn't have time to run across to the kitchens, from where he'd be able to escape. He was cornered in the dining hall. The only thing he could do was hide. So he slid under the nearest table and started crawling to the far right-hand corner of the room, sliding uncomfortably around the legs of tables. He reached the wall and leaned heavily against it. He heard something click.

The door to Kakophagy opened.

'I saw him come in here,' said Mrs Phipps.

'Check in the kitchens,' said Lady Anne. 'He might be hiding in there.'

Edward heard her footsteps approaching and pressed back even further. Lady Anne's perfume was advancing too – sweet and mystical, almost hypnotic. He held himself tightly against the wall, and suddenly he was falling backwards. A panel swung shut, closing him into a dark space. He heard Lady Anne coming closer, then stop, move the benches back, and turn away. He breathed out and looked around him. It was completely black. He felt around. The space was quite large – large enough for a full-grown man to sit in. He put his hand out tentatively and felt the rough stone of the wall behind him, his hand contracting when it touched something mossy or wet.

It was a tunnel. He let his hand run up the wall on his side, which was remarkably smooth, and felt the roof of it about half a foot above his head as he crouched. He wasn't able to stand up. He hoped it led somewhere. Then he remembered – it must be the secret passage that he had spent so long looking for when he was younger, that had been rumoured to take spies and monks to the church.

The church – that must be a safe place, he thought. Nothing evil could happen in a church.

He started crawling on his hands and knees. He wished that he had some sort of light. The air was dank and caught in his throat. He crawled faster, scraping his knees on the slimy stone, bumping his head. The darkness was beginning to clear a little, as his eyes adjusted themselves, but the tunnel was claustrophobically narrow. In the gloom he could hear many strange noises, but dismissed them. He kept going.

He heard a louder scuttling behind him. It was such an odd sound that he stopped. He could not see any light ahead of him. He moved again, and the scuttling came, faster this time. Edward crawled more quickly. And then the scuttling noise became a scraping, and he felt something grabbing his leg. It was hard, and cold.

He was frozen with terror for a moment, then kicked his leg out sharply, and was surprised to find that there was no weight on it. He looked back over his shoulder.

It was like nothing he had ever seen before.

A creature. It was made out of earth, it seemed, and twigs, and bits of stone and litter and grass. It extended itself. It was attracting everything in the tunnel to it. Moss detached itself from the walls and stuck on to it. Little stones were drawn to it, bits of debris and dirt and dust.

Its grip was pitiless. Every time Edward pushed a bit off it created another limb, trapping him.

He kicked it off and scrambled further. He could make out light ahead of him, the outline of a square. It must be another panel, he thought. I've got to get to it.

But the creature was so strong it was pulling him back. There was a slope leading up to the light. Inch by inch he scrabbled, the creature elongating bits of itself further up his leg, now on his back, and he could feel it tickling his spine. He crawled up the slope and felt around the light. It *was* another panel. He pushed against it as hard as he could. It wouldn't move. A piece of plastic was turning itself into a noose around his neck now, and it was tightening.

For a moment he saw himself dead in the tunnel, picked over by worms and rats, the Other Book surviving him, yellowed and dirty, speaking more horrors than his bones could tell.

Then Edward gritted his teeth and pushed again. This time something loosened and the panel swung open. He crawled out hastily and slumped against the wall, panting and tearing at the plastic which had closed around his throat, coughing out the horrible taste that had settled in it. But he could feel it choking him, squeezing the last breaths out of him.

Edward grappled with it and threw it off.

But it re-formed, and twigs and rocks began to cover him. Still he fought, as his face turned blue, still he battled until he could breathe no more and his head was filling up with white light . . .

'Dear God, what is that!' said a voice, and somebody rushed across and pulled the panel shut, then said something in sonorous Latin. There was a piercing noise, and Edward was released, and felt the air rush into his lungs.

Somebody splashed liquid over him and the creature started to come apart, the various bits which had come together sinking away until there was nothing left but a pile of small stones, the plastic ring on top.

'Communion wine,' said the voice, going to the panel, opening it and throwing the rubbish back in. 'That should do it.'

As Edward came to he looked around. He ran a hand through his hair. It felt wet, and he realised he had cut his head on the roof of the tunnel. He relaxed a little. His knees were a mess.

'Well, Mr Pollock. I do find you in the oddest of places. Have you been burying something bigger this time? You're terribly dirty. I'll ring through to my wife.' The Reverend Smallwood picked up the receiver of an old dial phone and spoke into it.

Edward looked around him. He was in the vestry. Dusty cassocks were strewn everywhere. Old hymn sheets were mixed up with parish newsletters and school calendars; half-burned candles and forgotten prayer books lay on top of cases of Communion wine. Books with titles like *Ordo Judiciorum* and *Shelford on Tithes* lined the walls. The Reverend replaced the receiver and sat down in an old brown armchair. The stuffing was coming out of the right arm.

Edward said, with some difficulty, 'You've got to help me.'

'Hold on there,' said Smallwood, 'let's get you cleaned up first.' A few minutes passed in which the Reverend studied him closely. Edward did not say anything. The door to the vestry opened and Mrs Smallwood rushed in.

'Edward! What have you been doing to yourself?' she said, and swiftly sprayed him with iodine and bandaged him up. 'There now. All better. Have a chocolate.' She patted him on the head, and then leant in to kiss her husband on the cheek.

'See you tonight,' she said to the Reverend, and went out.

'Now, how, my dear boy, did you end up being chased by something like that, into my study?' said the Reverend. He had stayed remarkably composed. Maybe he knew there was a passage there, in case something terrible happened and the school had to be evacuated. Smallwood motioned to Edward to sit down. He perched on a stool, sweeping off some choral music.

'Something's going on – something evil.' Edward caught his breath and coughed. 'Evil' seemed to him to be the right word to use in a place like this.

He began to explain everything breathlessly. Smallwood remained calm throughout, staring just to Edward's right, at a small crucifix which stood on a table.

'So this . . . Other *Book* which you have been talking about. Where is it now?' said Smallwood, idly turning over a coaster on a table which was next to his armchair.

Edward paused, and then said, with confidence, 'It's inside me. I've absorbed it. I don't know how. It's weird, I know, but . . .' Edward stopped talking.

There was a long silence. Smallwood regarded him with great interest, his eyes suddenly as cold as a dead fish.

'The Other Book . . . yes . . . yes . . . yes . . .' he muttered. 'I think . . . I think that this is it . . .'. His eyes were glinting slightly and his shuddering almost seemed as if it were from pleasure. 'It has that property, yes . . .' His tone changed. 'Of course, Pollock, if you had told me about this earlier then we could have saved an awful lot of trouble, couldn't we?'

The Reverend got up from his chair and paced across the room. Edward felt enclosed, embattled.

'There are more things in heaven and earth, Pollock, than are dreamt of in our philosophy. And I have dealt with a *lot* of them. Will you excuse me for a second. I made a promise to someone.' He went over to the phone, picked up the receiver and dialled. He whispered something into it and then replaced it with a strange grin on his face.

'And now, for this, Pollock, I thank you. You were meant to find it. Maybe you are like Galahad – too pure to see the darkness when it comes to you.'

Edward was unnerved.

'And you will be with me. You have a connection with it. This is something we must explore . . . It has to come out of you.' He put his hand on a heavy crucifix. 'It is a shame I don't know how . . .

'I had been looking for the sign for years, and then it came. When I saw you with the raven on a de la Zouche tomb. And with it . . . Oh, Edward! I had heard about it when I was just a boy, of eighteen. I found a reference to it in a manuscript when I was reading theology at Cambridge. Of course I knew then that it was all I needed. The world is so full, Edward, of pain and fear. And I could stop it all! With this Book, I could control all minds, all thoughts . . . The glory of heaven on earth, Edward! Everyone, calm, beautiful, worshipping our Creator! I had to become a lawyer to earn enough for my researches, but it has paid off in the end . . .'

It sounded like a nightmare to Edward.

The vicar advanced towards him, and put his hands on the boy's head. 'What are you doing?' said Edward, startled.

'Looking,' said the vicar, and closed his eyes.

Edward tore away, taking Smallwood by surprise, and banged at the panel. It wouldn't open.

'Oh, the spring for that is hidden very carefully,' Smallwood said. 'Do calm down, old chap.' The Reverend moved towards him, as if to comfort him, but Edward feared him. As Smallwood made to grab him, Edward performed a little dodge and slipped past him, making for the door.

'Good afternoon,' said a cool, elegant voice. Lady Anne stepped into the vestry through the door that led from the church.

'Lady Anne,' said the Reverend, composing himself.

'Thank you for letting me know about this.' She turned to Edward. 'You will come with me.' She took hold of his arm and led him through the church, calling back to Smallwood that she would speak with him later.

Pictures of saints looked down on them, keeping

their inscrutable thoughts to themselves. Lady Anne marched out through the church into the graveyard, pulling Edward behind, gripping his arm so tightly it hurt. She said nothing more, but she moved quickly and with grace.

The cemetery was full of noises and movement, of birds singing, the rustle of bushes in the slight breeze, the low-level droning of bees. The blazing heat made sweat bead on Edward's forehead. Lady Anne stopped by the de la Zouche monument. Edward's raven had long since gone from it, removed by the sexton.

'Sit there,' she said. Sheep bleated in the distance. Edward didn't move.

'Sit there,' she said again, and this time her voice compelled him. He scrabbled up and sat in the exact centre of the monument, where he had knelt before with the raven. The air was full of strange moanings carried from far away on the wind. The trees, though, were silent, watching. The thick air was like a blanket and Lady Anne's voice cut straight through it.

'Edward,' she said. He looked away. 'Please, Edward. Look at me.'

Reluctantly, he moved his eyes to her face, and felt the full force of her charm. He picked up some dead flowers, but they fell apart in his hands, dry and withered, as soon as he touched them.

'The Book,' she said. 'It is inside you. I want it. Give it to me.'

'I don't know what you're talking about. I don't know anything about it.' He didn't know how to get it out of him.

'You know what I'm talking about. Look at Bartlett, Lane Glover . . .'

'I don't know.' He glanced around to see where he could run. They were very close to the gate that led to the Manor. The gate, set in its old stone walls. Once he was through it, he thought, he would only be a few yards from Mr Fraser's office. Unlike the raven he could fly away. I'm not broken yet, thought Edward.

'Edward. Let me tell you something.' Lady Anne leant in confidentially. 'I have been looking for this for a long, long time now. Longer even than you have been alive. Since . . . well, since I was your age, really,' she said, remembering the night she had first seen Wentlake's portrait and felt the draw of his power. 'It is such a beautiful thing, Edward. So perfect and so right. It belongs to Oldstone Manor. And the Manor belongs to me.'

She continued, 'I had a feeling that it might come to a boy. There are reasons for that. It had to be an untouched mind, a pure mind. Galahad, indeed!' she laughed. 'A maiden!'

A *maiden*, thought Edward. *What does she mean?* He saw a brooch in her hair glint like a star.

'And you did my work for me . . . they knew that I would find it eventually, that I would want to restore it to its powers under Wentlake. One of my ancestors tried to tell me of the horrors that would happen to me if I used the Other Book in the wrong way. But I *despise* such weakness. I should have known it would be you when I found you on the drive. I should have taken you then, but you slipped from my grasp. Now one thing stands in my way, and that is you. The Other Book, dear Edward, has chosen you as its vessel. *I can feel it inside you.* But you know that it is rightfully mine. You can either stand with me or fall by yourself.'

'I don't believe you.' Edward felt the coolness of the tombstone through his shorts. He was seeking out a chink in her armour, just as Tristram would have done with an enemy knight. Seek out the weakness and aim for it, hard and true.

'Don't you? You have been dealing with powers stronger than you've ever known, Edward. You saw what I have done. I control Oldstone Manor, Edward, and much beyond it. Just try and break free. Just try.'

This was the moment. She relaxed, confident. Edward sprang off the other side of the monument. He scudded through the cemetery, jumping over the smaller graves, dashing round the bigger ones, and hurtled through the gate. He skidded to a halt in the courtyard. There was only one place to go, one person he could talk to – sensible, safe Mr Fraser. He ran to the door and banged on the glass panes.

'Mr Fraser! Sir! Sir! It's very important! Mr Fraser, sir!'

Fraser hurried to the door, unlocked it and let him in.

'What on earth are you doing out here, Pollock? It's late. You should be in the dorms by now.'

'Sir . . . sir, it's very important.'

'Sit down, Pollock, quickly. Spit it out.'

Edward did as he was told, but could barely contain himself.

'Lady Anne . . .' He coughed. 'She . . . she's plotting to overthrow you, sir!'

There was a big pause.

'I'm sorry, Pollock? Could you say that again?'

'She's plotting to overthrow you, sir! She's going to take over the school, and then when she's done that, God knows what she'll do!'

Mr Fraser sighed. 'Pollock, what are you talking about? I have better things to deal with than listen to you ranting and raving about plots.'

Edward remembered that Will had seen the Other

Book, had felt its influence, had seen it play out his thoughts. 'Ask Strangore! He knows!'

'Am I wasting my time, Pollock? Or will Strangore be able to throw some light on the matter?'

'Sir, please, you really need to hear this,' Edward pleaded.

'All right, then, Pollock,' Mr Fraser said, picking up the phone abruptly and dialling an extension. 'Mrs Ferrers . . . yes, could you send Strangore down to me here please? Immediately? Thank you.' He replaced the phone in its cradle.

Edward writhed with frustration, every second seeming too long. Two or three minutes later, during which Mr Fraser tapped furiously at his computer, there was a knock on the door. It was Will. Edward looked around and saw his cousin standing, owlishly, in the doorway.

'Strangore, come in, do.'

Will looked pale and nervous. He was in his pyjamas and clutching a toothbrush. He was still wearing his glasses. 'Sir?' He stood at the entrance.

'Strangore. Sit down.' Will sat down on a rickety chair that was on the other side of the room from Edward. Mr Fraser put his arms behind his head and clasped his hands together. 'What do you know about a conspiracy, Strangore?' His voice was gentle. Will looked puzzled, and shook his head.

'Conspiracy, sir?'

'Yes, Strangore. Conspiracy. Pollock here tells me that you might be able to throw some light on the matter.'

Edward looked intently at his cousin. He watched as Will hesitated, before saying, 'I . . . I don't know, sir.'

Edward was shocked. He didn't know that Will was ashamed, confused. He couldn't believe that Will didn't do the noble thing, the right thing. Edward couldn't see how he looked to Will, hair wild, eyes strange, covered in stains, his face bloody and his clothes torn. Edward looked at his friend imploringly, not realising that this made him look even madder.

'What don't you know, Strangore?' Mr Fraser inquired.

'I don't know anything, sir. I know that Edward read a book and thought that something bad happened because of it, but that's all, sir.'

'Thank you, Strangore. You may go back to your dorm,' said Mr Fraser.

Edward watched as Will backed out of the room, without having acknowledged him at all.

'Is this true, Pollock? Is this something you read in a book? Now tell me the truth. What happened?'

Edward gulped. He began to tell Fraser everything

he knew, right from the beginning.

When he had finished Mr Fraser looked at him gravely. 'Well, Edward. I'm not sure how seriously I can take any of this. I shall have to talk to Lady Anne.'

'No need, Headmaster,' said Lady Anne. She had come up slowly from the churchyard, and had been waiting outside in the courtyard, where she could hear everything. She moved in from the doorway. 'I think I can explain. Edward, we know, is a highly sensitive boy – he is given to, shall we say, fantasising? I think that you got specially frightened, today, didn't you Edward? And it all came tumbling down on you and you cooked up this little dream. Now come on, Edward. You know that I'm right.'

Edward shook his head. 'I'm telling the truth, sir.' He stayed silent and strong, remembering Tristram. His eyes were blazing and his voice didn't waver.

'Edward, this is a very strange story. If you would just admit that you made it all up, we can forget all about it, and we'll write this one off, shall we? You'll have a clean slate from tomorrow. This isn't the first time you've made things up, is it?'

Edward, trembling, turned towards the headmaster.

'Can you show us this book, Edward?' said Mr Fraser.

'No,' said Edward, frustrated. 'I can't.'

'Why not?' asked Fraser.

'It's . . . oh God, you won't believe me . . . it's sort of absorbed itself into my mind!' He looked at Mr Fraser beseechingly.

'There, you see,' said Lady Anne. 'He's admitted it!'

'Edward, are you lying? Lying is a terrible thing, you know,' said Mr Fraser. 'Tell us the truth, Edward.'

'The truth is what I've told you!' Anxiety clogged up his throat.

The phone rang. Mr Fraser answered. 'Oh botheration,' he said. He looked tired. 'I'll do it now, yes.' He fiddled with a pen. 'OK.' He put the phone down. 'Right, I have to go out for a bit. I'll be back in five mins. Anne, would you mind looking after Edward?'

'No!' said Edward. Things were going beyond his control. Mr Fraser's brow wrinkled, and he leant back in his chair, making it creak. The computer beeped again.

'Look, Edward, don't be silly. I'll be back in a jiffy.' He got up and left the room, leaving Edward alone with Lady Anne.

Edward felt the scuttling around his vision, the sensation that the boundaries of the world were thinning. He felt as if some greater presence were taking control over him, and that he was at one with the world; he felt that he was at the centre of the universe, and that everything flowed from him.

His vision cleared. A voice spoke. It was Lady Anne's. 'Let's just put you somewhere where I can look at you for a while. I'll enlist Doctor Spawforth.'

Afterwards he could only recall rushing and bustling; he remembered being carried, and a bed, a cool, soft bed; a huddle of concerned faces: they changed, often, sometimes they were recognisable, sometimes Tristram de la Zouche was there, looking down at him; sometimes totally alien faces were ringed round his vision; sometimes his mother and his father were there, and his brothers and sisters; there were doctors, lights, injections and the cold; and then nothing.

And then he woke up in a strange room. He looked around. It was wide and bright and the curtains were floral-patterned. There were flowers in a bowl filled with light on the table too, but someone had forgotten to replenish the water and they were nearly dead. There was a small television and a video player in the corner, and a stack of new videos. There were no books.

The window was open. There were bars on it. Edward looked at his watch. It was three o'clock in the afternoon.

I must have been asleep all night and all morning, he thought.

He moved to get up. Nothing seemed to be broken or otherwise wrong with him. He went to the window and looked out. He was high up. There was a garden below, which looked a long way away. He shuffled to the door and tried it. It was locked. Edward was trapped.

Twelve

feeling of failure bubbled inside Edward, spilling over into tears, which he managed to stop. He pulled himself together. He had to find a way out, consider the options.

He looked gloomily around the room again, and sat back down on the bed. He was wearing his own pyjamas and his own washbag was on the table. This made him feel better, somehow. It was good to see things that belonged to him.

He lay back and stared at the ceiling. There were no cracks in it. The lights were little spotlights, set into small recesses. The room had been painted a calming shade of light blue.

Someone opened the door, and the peace of the room was disturbed by shouts that seemed very near. A nurse entered and closed the door briskly, and the room was quiet again.

The nurse was young, with brownish hair. She smiled rogueishly at Edward as she came in. She was carrying a tin tray with a glass and two small white tablets in a little round dish.

'Good afternoon, Edward,' she said. 'How are you feeling?'

'I'm fine,' he said, shortly.

'Very good,' she said, putting the tray down on a small table.

'Where am I?' Edward sat up.

'You're in St Clive's Hospital,' said the nurse.

'How long have I been here?' he asked.

The nurse sat beside Edward on the bed.

'Two days,' she said.

Edward started up violently.

'There's no need to worry,' she said.

'Worry! But Lady Anne – I have to stop her!'

'Ssssh, there, it's all right,' said the nurse, offering Edward the pills. 'Why don't you drink these down and you'll feel a lot better.'

Edward looked at her suspiciously. 'What are they?'

'They're just something to help you sleep,' said the nurse. 'You haven't been properly diagnosed yet. You've been a little overexcited recently. You need a lot of rest, and then you'll be fine.'

Taking the pills from her and gulping them down,

Edward said, 'What's wrong with me?'

'The doctor says you might have temporal lobe epilepsy. He says you had a fit at school. They're going to run some tests on you. Don't worry, it's not as bad as it sounds.'

'What is it?'

'It's when you have a seizure, and you experience hallucinations – sounds, smells, a feeling of great intensity.'

Edward slumped back into his pillows. He knew he wasn't ill. He looked at the nurse, and wondered if he could make her his ally. 'What's your name?'

'Amy,' said the nurse. 'You know you've been talking a lot in your sleep.'

'What sort of things have I been saying?' asked Edward.

'Oh, nothing *incriminating*,' she said, with a slight lift of her eyebrows. 'I just wondered who Mandy might be?' Her nose crinkled slightly, and she gave Edward a sideways look.

Mandy! thought Edward. She seemed to belong to a different place. He remembered her, the day of the drinks party, laughing and joking in the courtyard. Tangled memories unravelled. The walls of the room around him seemed to be shivering, and Amy's voice was slowly morphing into Mandy's, and then it wasn't

Mandy at all, but someone else . . . and as he slipped away into sleep he heard groans, snatches of wild conversation coming from nearby . . . *His beak claps sidewise*, something shouted, and Edward had a vision of a long-haired, cackling creature . . . and then Amy wasn't there any more, and neither was the room.

Edward was in a peaceful forest glade. It was warm and the sunlight filtered through the leaves. The trees were dancing gracefully, and with a smile he recognised that the spirits of the wood were there, and that they were welcoming him. He wandered through the trees, and there in a small clearing was Tristram de la Zouche.

He was seated on the ground, and he wore his suit of gilded armour. His shapely, well-exercised horse was grazing to one side, its green and gold caparisons jingling softly as it moved. They were embellished with little embroidered ravens.

'Tristram!' said Edward, and ran to him. 'I've failed you and the line of Merlin . . . I've been captured by Lady Anne!'

Edward knelt down and stared at the grass, shame burning his cheeks. The knight touched his shoulders.

'Soft, soft, dear sir,' he said. 'Rise, my gentle squire.'

Edward rose up, and stood before him.

'You might think a dolorous thing has happened. You see no end to your suffering. You are languishing in gaol, as many a worshipful knight before you has done. Even Lancelot and the great Gawain were taken prisoner.'

'I wish it was all over.' Edward's feelings were coming up from the depths of his mind.

'You should not wish that,' said Tristram sternly. 'The Other Book is a part of you and your destiny, and you cannot change that. Remember this – whilst it and its powers are in you, those who seek it cannot use it. Lady Anne . . .' He trembled, and smote his fist upon the ground. 'I curse my descendent! That such ignominy should fall upon so great a house!'

Edward watched him as he struggled with his anger. When Tristram turned back to Edward, his face was calm.

'It hurts to hold it,' said Edward quietly.

'If there were not deeper reasons, it would have destroyed you by now.'

'Why does Lady Anne want it?' asked Edward.

'Because she is of the line. She desires to be as Wentlake de la Zouche. She thinks that he achieved the sublime. She will try to take it from you. Both she and the Reverend will assail you sorely. But you must resist – and fight back, and overcome.'

'Tell me what to do,' said Edward.

'I wish that I could, gentle child,' said Tristram. 'But it is not for me to do so.'

'But why?'

'Because I am only a messenger, as you well know. I have already overstepped the limits of my duties.'

'You saved me and Will, in the dorm?'

The knight nodded. He said no more.

'Why can't I stay here?'

'You cannot. Whilst you are in this state, you are dead to the world outside. Your body lies unconscious and vulnerable. If you did remain in this, your dream-world, too long, then you would perish. You must go back now,' he said.

There was noise, rushing, falling. An eternity of nothingness. Pricks of light in a blanket of shadow. Light expanding, filling the void, brightening until . . .

Edward was back in bed. It was nearly dark and the curtains were closed. He was alone. There was a clock above the blaring television, in the shape of a cartoon character. Its gloved hands were pointing to nine and six. Half past nine. Edward got out of bed and turned the television off. He went to the door and shook the handle. It clicked open. Amy must have left the door unlocked when she had left.

He slipped out on to a corridor, which stretched far

to the left and right, doors exactly like his own at equal intervals. He looked at his door – it was numbered 9E, and his name was written on a card in little black handwriting. There was a smell of soap and disinfectant, but underneath it the smell that nothing can ever get rid of – the smell of sickness, and death.

The glow of televisions came out from underneath doors, accompanied by disembodied voices. He edged out of the room. High-pitched laughter erupted from very near. A man was walking down the corridor, his hair long, his face like a saint in a painting, but he was making sounds that came from hell, raw, unquenchable groans. Edward shrank into the doorway, and waited till he went past.

Edward decided to go down the corridor as far as he could, to see if he could find a way out in the morning. He was sure that he could just discharge himself. If he went to the desk and explained that he was perfectly all right, then they'd let him out. They'd see that a mistake had been made. He could phone his parents and they'd come and rescue him.

There were no signs on the walls, so he did a quick 'eeny meeny miny mo' and chose to go left. It was cold, so he moved quickly. He made no sound as he padded down the corridors in his bare feet. He wished that he'd thought to put his slippers on. He went quietly through a pair of doors, and came upon the end of the corridor.

It opened out into what seemed to be a large common room. There were soft seats around the edges, a bean bag or two. There was a table-football table, at which four people were playing. The lights were thin and fluorescent and there was an ever-present television in a corner of the room. Green plastic chairs had been drawn up in front of it, and a few people were sitting down watching the programme that Edward had just switched off.

Nobody took any notice of him, so Edward inched down into one of the seats. He felt lonely, unwanted, lost. Come on, he said to himself. Don't give in now. He put his head in his hands. He could feel the depth of emptiness threatening to drown him. Don't let her win, he thought.

'Hey, are you all right?' said someone. Edward looked up. He saw a man with longish, curly brown hair looking down at him. He was wearing a blue and green striped jumper. He looked like he was in his early twenties. He had faint stubble, and staring eyes, a snub nose. He flicked his hair away with an impatient gesture. 'Mind if I sit down?'

Edward sat up, and shrugged. The man sat down. Edward smiled a little at him.

'Now,' said the man, 'we can have proper introductions. My name is Tom O'Bedlam.' Edward laughed quietly, but then stopped when he noticed that Tom looked pained.

'So what's it like round here?' he said.

'It's not too bad, really,' said Tom. 'The nurses are all really nice, and all the doctors are mostly cool, except for . . .' and he looked around, carefully, before whispering, '*Dr Spawforth*.'

The name rang a bell with Edward. Slowly, things started to come back to him and he recalled that Lady Anne had said it before he blacked out. So she definitely had something to do with this. He didn't really want to strike up a conversation with Tom. He was nervous. Escape was paramount.

'Where are you sleeping?' said Tom conversationally.

'9E,' said Edward, desperately trying to think of a way out. He didn't want to come up against this Spawforth if he had anything to do with Lady Anne.

'There's a weird guy a couple down from you. Got a son that visits him. *Very* strange. He is, I mean, not the son.'

No one spoke for a second. More cheers and whoops came from the television area.

'So, you look like the kind of man who could keep a

secret,' said Tom, in a confidential manner.

'Yeah, sure,' said Edward, irritated.

'If I tell you one, will you tell me one too?'

Edward looked around the room. There was another set of doors, as well as the one through which he'd come. None of the other residents looked friendly. They were all engrossed in the television.

'What's your secret, then?' said Edward, indifferent. Anything to get him off his back.

Tom spoke in a low, deep voice. Edward felt the lights in the room darken and the television sound quieten. He stiffened, a hare about to spring. Astonished, Edward watched as Tom began to swell, his limbs becoming longer, his whole body becoming larger.

'I am Tom O'Bedlam. I have been here since the beginning, and I will be here at the end. Where there is madness I walk, where there is lunacy I stalk. I am Tom O'Bedlam and *this is my house*.'

The lights came up again and Tom was the same size he had been before. Edward got up, swiftly. 'Well, it was nice to meet you,' he said, too quickly, his heart beating loudly. 'I must be going now.'

'Don't go now,' said Tom. '*You promised*.'

The cheering in the room got much louder. Tom O'Bedlam did nothing, but stared at Edward, contemptuously, and then Tom's face withered; and as if he were a mummy being unwrapped, the folds of skin seemed to fall off, and there, underneath the curls and the brown eyes was the malicious, expressionless face of Mrs Phipps.

Thirteen

dward backed away immediately. The creature raised a hand and he felt himself being dragged slowly towards it. He fought it and fought it, whilst the cheering went on blithely around him, and he was dragged closer and closer to that clammy skin.

'Didn't you, Pollock. *You promised me a* secret.'

Edward could feel the fevered, malodorous breath on his cheek and closed his eyes tightly, not wishing to see what lay in store.

'Edward! Are you all right?' It was the nurse's voice. 'You should get back to bed, now.'

And where Phipps had been standing there was nothing. 'OK,' said Edward. But he didn't want to go back to bed. There was no telling what he'd find there. He had to find a way out. He waited till Amy had gone out of the room. He was almost frantic.

He tried the set of doors on the opposite side of the room from where he had come in. They opened out into a wide reception area. He peered round the corner. A nurse was behind the reception desk. He was looking intently at a computer. The room was full of uncomfortable plastic chairs, another flickering television, and brightly coloured, slapdash paintings of things that looked like exploding suns and scorched landscapes. There were double doors to the right of the desk. Edward guessed that they led to the stairs and the lifts. The nurse was so engrossed in what he was doing that Edward wondered briefly if he could sneak out past him and to freedom. The nurse seemed to be playing a computer game, and Edward couldn't help thinking that that was exactly what he'd do when this was all over.

He was in his pyjamas, barefoot, he had no money, and didn't know where St Clive's was. The repugnance of seeing Mrs Phipps appear under Tom's friendly face returned to him. He tried to shake it from his mind by thinking about the situation and his plan to escape.

Even if he could find a taxi, he didn't have any money; if he phoned the police, they'd bring him straight back here. He wondered also if he could go up to the nurse anyway, and make friends with him. He looked amiable, young. He'd just decided to go up to the desk, when the double doors opened.

Nurse Amy came in, looking concerned. Her hair was drawn back into a ponytail and she kept fiddling with it. She was followed by Lady Anne and the Reverend Smallwood. Edward pressed back against the wall. They went up to the desk. The nurse looked up from his game, slightly apologetically.

'Hello. What can I do for you?' he said.

GAME OVER! said the computer, loudly. *GAME OVER! GAME OVER!*

That's exactly how I feel, thought Edward.

'Aww . . . sorry,' said the nurse, pressing something on the keyboard. 'How can I help you, love?'

'Good evening,' said Lady Anne in a steely voice which suggested that she had never been called 'love' before, and certainly didn't expect to be called so by a nurse. 'We have come to see Edward Pollock. He was admitted to your care two days ago. I am sure you remember him. He came from Oldstone Manor, on my recommendation.'

'Oh yeah, Edward Pollock, sent here on Lady Anne de la Zouche's recommendation.' He tapped some keys. 'It says here that no one except his family is allowed see him. And you're not his family, are you?'

'I've told them they can't,' said Amy, interrupting.

'It's very late and I've just sent Edward back to bed. He's too tired to see any visitors.'

Edward thanked her silently.

'I'm sure Edward would love to see us,' said the Reverend. Edward winced. 'We're practically family. I've known Edward for years. I am concerned about his spiritual health, and wish to comfort him in his sickness.'

'Yes,' said Lady Anne. 'And I am a close friend of his family.'

She's lying, thought Edward, and willed Amy and the nurse to see through her. But her spell was working.

'I have spoken to Dr Spawforth on the phone,' said Lady Anne. 'He said that of course we could see Edward. He was sure that such friends as we are could do nothing but help him.'

Death to Dr Spawforth, thought Edward.

The nurse looked at Amy. 'Is this true?' he said.

Amy nodded reluctantly. 'Yes. Although I've told Dr Spawforth that it would be very bad for Edward to have any visitors – any visitors at all, even those close to him. Why, he wouldn't let his best friend in to see him.'

Strangore had come. Edward hoped he was feeling guilty about leaving him in the study like that. Some best friend he'd turned out to be.

'Well, the doctor knows his own business,' said the nurse. 'What would you like to see him for?'

'We are so, so worried about poor Edward,' said Lady Anne. 'We just want to make sure that he's all right, and has everything that he needs.' Her charm was working upon the nurse, and he smiled at her, picking up a pen.

'Well, I can't see any problem in that, and since Dr Spawforth has approved, I'll put you down for half an hour tomorrow. From three o'clock?'

'Couldn't we make it a little earlier?' said the Reverend.

'Well, I don't know about that,' said the nurse. 'The boy needs his rest.'

'I think eleven o'clock will be fine,' said Lady Anne firmly. Edward could hear the persuasion in her voice.

'Eleven o'clock it is, then,' said the nurse, and scratched his head, slightly puzzled. The spell had worked.

I'll have to escape before then, thought Edward. But as he considered the doors through which Lady Anne had just gone, an orderly came through them. 'Time to lock up?' he said to the nurse. 'Yeah,' said the nurse, and the orderly advanced to where Edward was.

Edward slipped round and headed back towards his room. There was no point going out after Lady Anne.

She might still be waiting around. Nowhere was safe. He had to be on his guard all the time. Eleven o'clock tomorrow, he thought. He was glad he had come out into the hospital. He would be able to prepare himself for their visit. Whatever they tried to do . . . He shuddered thinking about it. They'd try to get the Other Book out of him. And it was part of him, now. How they were going to do that, he didn't even hope to guess. Something told him it wouldn't be much fun.

Fourteen

dward padded softly back down the corridor. He was a couple of doors away from his room. The orderly was moving very quickly, bearing down upon him, like a very slow elephant. He was marching down the corridor, not looking to left or right, swinging a bunch of keys. Edward couldn't risk being caught by him now. And who knew that it wasn't Mrs Phipps in disguise? He might bring me out to the reception area, thought Edward, where Lady Anne and the Reverend could still be lurking. There's only one thing for it, he thought, and ducked into the nearest room, closing the door behind him.

He was forced to shut his eyes, because it was so bright after the darkness of the corridor. Red shapes formed against his eyelids, and he cautiously opened them. A television was flickering gently in the corner.

He blinked for a moment, adjusting.

The room was the same size as his own, with a bed in the corner. A bed which contained a shape, that was stirring under the sheets. He hoped he hadn't disturbed the occupant. He stayed by the door, ready to spring out. He only had to wait a couple of minutes before the orderly went past.

This room was much more lived-in than Edward's. The walls looked like they hadn't been painted for a while. They were a deep, rich red. They were also covered with pictures – engravings of old buildings, diagrams, symbols. Papers were strewn all over the place – reams of writings in several different hands, piles of printouts on the brink of toppling over, and towers of old books with their covers coming off. An ancient, blackened chest, its lid propped open, was full of more books, tottering in piles, threatening to cascade to the ground.

The shape in the bedclothes sat up. It was a man, dark-haired, gaunt, unshaven, swarthy. The man Edward had seen earlier, walking down the corridor, with the face of a saint. He wore blue and pink striped pyjamas and there was a long scar going from his ear to his mouth. His hair was very long and greasy. His cheekbones were sharply prominent, and his nose straight. Even from across the room Edward could see that his eyes were a piercing dark blue. They focused on him.

'You. You've changed,' he said, slowly and deliberately.

Edward edged towards the door. 'I'm sorry,' he said. 'I didn't mean to –'

'No! Don't go. This is interesting. Why have you changed? Or rather, what is it that has changed you? I must set it down. My tables! My tables!' he laughed. He scrabbled around and picked up a small, black notebook, and scribbled in it. 'Met-a-mor-phos-is,' he said, enunciating every syllable. 'Haven't seen one of those for a while. You haven't been disobeying the gods, have you? Or are you running away from one?'

'No . . . no, sir,' said Edward.

He was nearer the door, and he reached out to put his hand on the doorknob.

'No!' said the man. 'Here. Stay here. I want to know why.'

He'd almost shouted the last bit. He was making too much noise. Edward didn't want him to create a disturbance. The orderly was probably still within earshot. Edward went closer to the bed.

'Ah . . . ah, yes, yes, come closer. What are you? A little tatterdemalion, a little flibbertigibbet. The foul fiend bites my back. So, young renegade, you have entered my realm.' He swept his arm around the room. 'And what is your name? Do you have one? Or has it changed too?'

'Edward, sir.' He couldn't think of a fake name. 'Edward Pollock.'

'Come closer, Edward Pollock. Let me look at this metamorphosis.'

Edward crept forward, stumbling through dusty piles of paper. He reached the man's bedside. He grabbed Edward's neck and pulled him so close that Edward could see the man's pores.

He spoke fiercely, right into his ear, his spittle covering Edward's cheek. 'What is inside you must be destroyed, my little one, for it is wrong, *all wrong*!'

Edward struggled against him, but couldn't get free, the man was crushing him tighter and tighter, and Edward shouted, and the door opened, and someone came in and said, 'What's going on? Dad, what are you doing?' And the man let Edward go.

Edward stepped back from the bed to find himself face to face with Guy Lane Glover. They stood looking at each other, Lane Glover's face going through a mixture of surprise, shame and hatred.

'So now there are two,' said the man, and pulled the bedclothes over his head. '*Two, of course there are two. It seems perfectly natural now – the one who never looks up, whose eyes are lidded and balled, like Blake's . . .'* He groaned like a banshee. What he said seemed familiar to Pollock, but made no sense.

'It's all right, Pa,' said Lane Glover. 'There's only one of me. It's OK.' The man pulled the blankets off his head again, and Lane Glover ran to him. He took the man's hand, and the man put his head against Lane Glover's chest.

'Pollock,' said Lane Glover. 'What are you doing here?' He wasn't angry, just sad.

'I'm . . . I'm sorry, Guy,' said Edward. 'I didn't know . . . your father, I'm sorry . . .'

'*I am red meat. His beak claps sidewise: I am not his yet!*' said Mr Lane Glover.

His beak claps sidewise . . . the image was horrible, and Edward had heard it before somewhere . . . was this another trap? he thought.

'What does he mean when he says that?' asked Edward.

'He's not mad,' said Guy. 'He isn't. He's quoting from something. Sylvia Plath. It's a poem.'

'I . . . I'm sorry, Guy,' said Edward, and Guy sighed, let go of his father's hand, and slumped down into the chair by the bed.

'*Somebody's done for,*' said his father.

'Sssh,' said Guy. 'It's all right. I'm here now.'

They were silent for a moment, as Guy comforted his father, and the low flicker of the television spluttered in the corner. Edward wondered if he had a mother, or any other family at all. He wondered why no one had come with him to the hospital. He would never have been allowed to make a journey like that on his own.

'How long has he been like this?' Edward asked.

'He's been here for three years now,' said Guy. 'He was a professor of English at University College in London, before.'

'What happened?' asked Edward.

'I don't really want to talk about it.' Guy sat on a chair and looked at his father. His father smiled. Guy let go of his hand and said, 'Well, I suppose since you're here, you might as well know everything that I know.' He got up, pushed some books off a chair, and Edward sat down in it. 'It's a long story. Dad used to be a great lecturer – he loved his job, and his students loved him. He was researching into some old documents, and it was all going fine – he was getting funding, and we were moving to a bigger house – until he became obsessed with something.

'I don't know what it was. He used to talk about something, about a book that would prove some theory he'd been working on. But he never found it, and one day he came home, and he was . . . like this.' He looked down at the floor. 'He admitted himself. Just wandered in here one day, and said, "I can't do it any more." And I was sent to Oldstone Manor, and my father stayed here...' He patted his father's hand again. 'So what are you here for, Pollock?' he said. 'Looking for a book too?'

'Well... it's funny you should say that. Promise not to think that I'm mad?'

Guy looked around the room, and shrugged. 'Knock yourself out,' he said. 'You're in the right place.'

So Edward told him everything that had happened. The television continued to flicker in the corner, its low voices sounding like they were spelling out some awful doom. The intense brightness of the lights showed up everything in the room, the papers, the diagrams, the books all glowing seemingly from the inside.

Glover paid attention to Edward, sometimes asking him to repeat something if he hadn't understood it. When he came to telling him about Strangore, O'Brien and the pond, Glover said, 'I wondered what got into me that day. Something just seemed to take me over.' Sometimes his father would surface from the half-sleep he had entered into. When Edward got to Reverend Smallwood, Guy's father sat up straight in bed.

'But that's it! That's it, my boy! It's here *somewhere*! I know it is!'

204

'Ssshh . . . be quiet,' said Guy. His father was more excited than usual, and took some calming down.

They talked long into the night. If you hadn't known that they were enemies, from the way that they spoke you might have thought that they were best friends. This was another side to Lane Glover, and Edward felt his dislike slipping away.

Guy told Edward that he and his mother had worshipped his father. He'd been like an enchanter, casting powerful spells of attraction on all those that came near him, the centre of a small group of charmed people – artists, poets, writers, models, politicians, lawyers, bankers, people whose talents and brains had brought them together. The house in Islington was large, and always full of visitors. Sometimes they stayed for months, sometimes they were gone in an hour. His father was eccentric, always, and inclined to be obsessive. But Lane Glover had loved him all the more for his oddities.

And then one day he had come home from a visit somewhere, and had not been able to speak properly. He'd sung in snatches of madness and half-remembered quotes. And then he had broken down. He had admitted himself to St Clive's that day.

Around midnight Edward decided to go to bed. Lane Glover promised he'd try to see him the next day.

'Pollock,' he said, as he was leaving the room.

'What?'

'I believe you.'

'What?' said Edward. This wasn't like Lane Glover. Although admittedly he now knew he hadn't known what Lane Glover was like.

'I believe you. Look what a book did to my father. I think I'd believe anything after that.'

'Thanks,' said Edward. 'Where are you going to sleep?'

'I sleep here, some nights. Now that I'm on suspension. There's a camp bed.'

'No bedbugs?'

'No.' The two boys stood in silence for a moment. 'Thanks, Edward,' said Guy. 'Let's talk in the morning.'

Edward left Guy and his father and stole back into his room. He hoped fervently, as he slipped back into his bed, that he had made an ally. He needed all the help he could get. Edward fell gently into natural sleep.

He was dreaming quietly of green and gold forests when there was a tremendous crash and he jumped out of sleep. Somebody – or something – had knocked over his chair and was creeping towards him. In the murky light he couldn't make out what it was – it seemed oddly shaped. He stiffened and tried to get up, but the shape leapt at him and something was placed firmly over his mouth. In his half-sleep it was difficult to struggle, but he tried. He couldn't move his arm. His brain was paralysed. Though he was sending urgent messages to his limbs, they just wouldn't budge. It felt like he was swimming in treacle.

The door creaked open and a thin shaft of light fell on to the floor. An orderly poked his head around it.

The thing on his bed wasn't making any noises. He tried to shout. The orderly closed the door, and he was plunged into darkness again.

Whatever it was pulled Edward's pillow out from under his head and started to press it down upon him. He kicked and kicked – it seemed curiously light and he hoped he could kick it off. He screamed inside – he was finding it harder and harder to breathe.

The pillow was taken off him and something brushed his face. It felt disgusting, alive, clammy, leathery and cold, and it stroked his face, and he was aware of a low whistling sound, endless, inhuman, dry and meaningless, like an insect's noise. Squeezing his eyes shut he fought against it more and, as he kicked, the door opened again. Whatever it was suddenly released him.

Edward heard the click of the switch and heard something laughing. He opened his eyes. Mrs Phipps was sitting on his bed, glaring down at him, radiating malevolence. For a moment she looked like a beast with fangs and leathery wings, then she morphed back into her usual shape. He recoiled and tried to get out of the bed, but couldn't.

Then a voice spoke – one Edward didn't recognise. Mrs Phipps melted backwards. The voice was metallic, rasping. 'So this is the subject,' it said. 'We'll have to see what we can do.'

Edward sat up in bed. He noticed that the clock above the door said seven thirty. A little man was standing in the centre of the room. He was almost entirely bald. He looked like he had never had any hair. He wore a shabby brown suit and carried a clipboard. Edward thought there was something menacing about clipboards.

'Well, Edward Pollock,' said the man. 'Let me introduce myself. I am Doctor Isocrates Spawforth.'

Spawforth, thought Edward. Help. Not someone to mess around with. Edward might have guessed that standing behind the doctor was Lady Anne. She was wearing a summery, floating dress that was entirely at odds with her expression. A long chain of beads dangled around her neck, which she was twisting as she came forward.

'I can't tell you how *useful* Phipps has been,' she

said. The ghastly creature, human now, shuffled to her mistress and cackled. Behind her was Reverend Smallwood.

'Let's get to the point,' said Lady Anne. 'Strap him in.'

Two heavy-looking orderlies in bright white coats came forward and strapped Edward down into the bed, then wheeled him out into the centre of the room. He shouted, 'Help!' But then he realised how stupid that was. Dr Spawforth was in charge, after all.

The bed had wheels, and one of the orderlies pushed it out into the middle of the room. 'Follow me,' came the metallic voice. Spawforth marched ahead. As they went past Guy's father's room Edward yelled, '*I am not his yet!*' It was something Guy's father had said, and he hoped Guy would realise that something was wrong.

But nobody came out of the door.

Edward was pushed down the passageway, Spawforth marching ahead all the time, Lady Anne and the Reverend behind him. Through the double doors, into the main reception area of the ward, into a large lift and then up. He didn't see which floor they were taking him to. It was certainly two or three stops. Nobody else got into the lift.

The orderly pushed him out again, down more bleak corridors, through more doors, past bleary-eyed nurses and unfocused patients, and finally they came to a stop in a large room.

It was an operating theatre. There was a trolley full of instruments, a table, a huge lamp. Suddenly he remembered the day of the drinks party at Oldstone Manor, when he had looked out of the window at the tables being prepared below, and for a second it had seemed as if he were being examined on them. That had been a foreshadowing of this moment, and Edward realised that he should have paid attention. Again he felt a tightening, as of a bow-string, again he felt powerless, a puppet being dangled over an abyss.

'What are you going to do?' he said. He tried to speak as firmly as he could.

'There is something, Edward, that is lurking inside you. The Other Book,' said Lady Anne, 'has sucked itself into your cells, into the very marrow of your bones. And it is beyond my reach. So, with the help of Dr Spawforth and his *machine* here, I hope to get it out of you. Sometimes, we must have necessary recourse to Science, Edward. That is something you will learn. If there is anything left of you. We are going to *rip* it out of you, Edward. This machine can mimic the power that I have. It will serve, instead of the other person I need. And that is all I need to get it out of you. Ready?'

There was a large contraption in the corner of the

room. If it had been flashing and buzzing strangely, Edward wouldn't have minded so much, but there was something terrible about the clinical silence with which it was turned on and put into position.

Spawforth turned on a dictaphone and started speaking. 'Subject: Edward Pollock, twelve-year-old male. Time 0742 hours.'

The machine was manoeuvered next to the bed. Edward squirmed in his straps but they were too tight. There was only one thing to do, and that was to lie still. The machine had a giant tube attached to it, which had an opening about the size of his chest. It was lowered slowly until it was about twenty inches above him. And then a button was pressed, and a little disc came out, and the disc was covered in tiny, sharp, glinting hooks. And it started moving up and down.

Edward couldn't help it. He screamed. His thoughts were not, at that time, on escape. He thought he'd had it. He felt the Other Book shrieking in its strange syllables through his curdling brain. It knew what was happening. The fact that it couldn't help Edward, or didn't want to, was horrible.

The whole time, the metallic voice of Dr Spawforth was scraping in the background.

'Subject seems to be experiencing fear.'

The little disc was being lowered to his chest. He felt

the tiny hooks scrape his skin and there was a plunge and Edward kept telling himself, don't scream, don't scream, and he didn't.

And then the tube retracted. Edward could feel blood welling out of his chest. He couldn't sit up, he was strapped so tightly. There was a commotion of some sort going on.

'Christ! What is that!' said someone.

'What are they doing in here? Get them out!'

'Phipps, why aren't you doing anything?'

Edward could make out confused rustling noises. Then he heard Lady Anne saying, 'You! You remember . . . you remember how to . . . Damn you, Ferdy!'

'Edward, are you OK?' Someone leant over him. It was Guy. He quickly unstrapped Edward. Mrs Phipps wafted over to him, slowly revealing black and brown teeth. Edward could see Lady Anne, furious. She looked trapped.

Mr Lane Glover ran to the bed, and Mrs Phipps flew from it as if she were made from muslin, and billowed away. Guy shrank back as she passed.

'Urgh!' He put his hand over his nose and mouth. 'Get out!'

'You don't have to tell me that,' Edward said, and leapt off the bed.

'Come on!' said Guy. 'Follow me!' He ran to his

father, and Edward with him. Mr Lane Glover was concentrating very hard, and a light was shining from him. Phipps floated towards them once more, but Edward saw that she was repulsed by the light.

'Hold off! Hold off!' shouted Guy's father. He was straining. Doctor Spawforth was rooted to the spot; he looked terrified. Lady Anne was seething. She said a few words which made the light dim, but Mr Lane Glover responded by making it brighter. 'Now! Go!' he shouted, and the two boys ran out as the light got so bright it was blinding. Edward didn't stop to wonder how Lady Anne had known Guy's father. And neither, for that matter, did Guy.

Fifteen

r Lane Glover followed the boys out of the operating theatre. He pulled the doors to, and to Edward's relief nothing came out after him.

'I knew it!' said Guy's father. 'Now come on. We haven't got much time. They won't try anything again for a bit.' They all raced down the corridor.

'What were you *doing* in there, Dad?' said Guy.

'Getting the foul fiend off my back,' replied his father. 'This is kind of hard for me to explain. I . . . we . . . we used to mess around, a lot, with things that we didn't really understand. Old books . . . powers. Not magic, because it isn't. It's more getting to know how the world works and then learning how to bend the rules a little . . . There are forces that you can manipulate. I just learned how to do that.'

'Dad, that's awesome! Why don't you do it more often?'

'You shouldn't do it for your own gain, Guy, that's something I learned very quickly, but something that –' Mr Lane Glover stopped, and didn't seem to want to carry on.

'Never mind. You all right, Pollock?' said Guy as they ran.

'I'm fine,' Edward panted.

'I knew it!' said Guy's father, again.

They ran through the corridors and into the lifts. As the doors closed behind them, they caught their breaths.

Guy turned to Edward. 'My dad's got a lot to tell you.'

The lift came down to their floor. The passage was empty. It was early morning, sunlight filtering through the windows as if nothing had happened. The sounds of the hospital waking up could be heard – trolleys being trundled, nurses saying cheery good mornings. They slipped quietly into Mr Lane Glover's room. It was even messier than it had been earlier.

Mr Lane Glover was in his towelling dressing gown. Guy spoke. 'When you went to bed, Dad was really upset, and spent ages scrabbling around. I heard you shouting. *I am not his yet.* Something Dad said. I guessed something was up. I scoped out the corridor

215

and saw them pushing you away, and Dad looked out and saw Lady Anne and he went *crazy*. We came after you as fast as we could . . .'

'This Book that you've told Guy about,' said his father. '*It's what I was looking for*.' He tightened his dressing gown.

'So you know all about it?'

'Everything in this room is a result of my research . . . it's all here.'

'So do you know what the Other Book does?'

'Yes,' said Guy's father. He flapped his arms, a hawk on a falconer's wrist. He told how the Other Book was used to influence the pattern of history and bring about the greater glory of mankind. It was the source of power of the de la Zouches. It was intertwined with them, part of their genetic coding. Years touched with gold hung around the Manor, from Saxon times before the Conquest, until the days of Charles II. All – except one – used it wisely, bringing beauty, knowledge, science and song to the land, keeping a small enclave of light even when all else was dark around.

But its other use – and its most important use – was against the creatures of the Other World, that howls around ours. The de la Zouche family was destined to guard the boundaries, the price they paid for the Other Book.

Wentlake had thought that he could merge the two worlds. He believed that there was a greater power in the Other World, which he would be able to control. He had gone far towards furthering his aim, but Merlin had prevented him at the last minute.

'How do you know all this, Mr Lane Glover?' said Edward.

'Ferdinand, please. Believe me, I've read a lot about it. Funny that it was you . . . I remember something about a maiden finding it . . .' He rooted around again. 'Now come on. We should get going.' He went behind a Chinese screen. The dressing gown appeared, flung over the top, and then his pyjamas. 'Guy, hand me my clothes!' Guy rushed to give them to him.

'And how does Lady Anne fit in?' said Edward.

Ferdinand stiffened at the name. 'There is a poem by Tennyson in *Idylls of the King*, which started it all off for us . . . for me. It's about Merlin and Vivien, and how Merlin was trapped in a tree for eternity by the enchantress.'

'I know it!' The poem rose from a dusty fold of Edward's mind. He remembered that day by the river when Lady Anne read it to them. '*Thou read the book, my pretty Vivien! . . . O ay, it is but twenty pages long . . . And every square of text an awful charm . . . And every margin scribbled with comment . . . And none can read the text, not even I; and none can read the comment but myself.'*

'That's right!' said Ferdinand, pulling on his trousers. 'The book in the poem is the Other Book. But how did you come across the Book?'

Up till now Edward had kept it secret. It was a wrench for him. Talking to a dream knight is good evidence for lunacy. To his surprise, when he told them about Tristram de la Zouche, they didn't even flinch.

Instead, Ferdinand seemed deliriously happy. 'I came across him, too,' he said. 'But only in a manuscript. And you've been in direct contact with him . . . this is wonderful!' He gave another whoop, and kicked his heels together. Guy looked at him and rolled his eyes, but he seemed a lot happier now. 'But why didn't you say this earlier? What did he tell you?'

'He said it was my destiny to guard the Other Book, and to return it to the rightful owner.'

'And did he tell you who that was?'

Edward shrugged. 'Beats me.'

'Well, they're certainly hiding themselves from Lady Anne. Right, we'll have to get this sorted out now. Let's go.' Edward noticed him looking pensively at Guy, who was lying on the bed on his back with his head hanging down to the ground.

Ferdinand was filled with a new purpose. His madness had evaporated.

'We've got to get you out of here. We've got to carry out your task. Merlin and Vivien chose the Manor as a stronghold from where the Other Book could be used by their descendants – the Guardians. That is where we must go. In fact,' he said, struggling with a tie, 'the oak tree at the Manor had the same parent as the one Vivien trapped Merlin in. It was planted as a reminder of Vivien's seduction of Merlin, to warn all future Guardians against excess. For they both transgressed.'

Edward remembered *Idylls of the King* – the old wizard letting his emotions get the better of him, the seductress allowing her power-lust to take over.

'They realised that there has to be a balance. So they poured their powers together. And now we must restore that power.'

Edward didn't say that Tristram had left it up to him, that he was only a messenger from someone or something else. For the first time in his life he had felt truly powerful, with this magic in him. It didn't bother him that it was someone else's power. It would be hard to get rid of it. It would be painful for Lady Anne to get the Other Book out of him. It would be even more painful to see it given away or destroyed.

'Right,' said Ferdinand, throwing Edward an old

jumper, 'I'll distract the nurse, and you two can slip out. Run and hide in the car. Here are the keys, OK?'

The boys nodded. Ferdinand cast his eyes around the room. 'I can come back for all this later.' He looked at himself in the mirror. He looked so different from when Edward had first seen him that it was hard to believe it was the same person.

They stepped out into the corridor. It stretched out on either side, empty. The only noises were the continual whine of the televisions, and the laughing of the inmates. It was half past eight. Ferdinand strode on ahead, confident, radiating sanity. He burst through the double doors and marched up to the desk. Another nurse had replaced the one Edward had seen before.

'Good morning,' said Guy's father. 'How are you?' He asked her something which made her bend over the computer. Guy and Edward took the opportunity to slide round to the doors which led to the stairs. They were just going to burst through them when the doors flew open and Lady Anne and the Reverend stormed in. They were squashed against the wall behind the doors. Edward felt slightly ill.

'And look! There is Ferdinand Lane Glover himself.' Lady Anne was restrained, coiled. Her wrist flashed with jewels, points of light gathered at her throat. The boys held on to the door like limpets.

Ferdinand turned round, and with mock servility, said, 'My Lady. How lovely to see you again.' He reached out and took her hand, and she let him lower his lips to it, then retracted it slowly.

'You have something of mine,' said Lady Anne.

'OK,' said Edward quietly. 'On the count of three . . . One . . . two . . .' and on three he and Guy slid out and ran for it, banging the door behind them.

'And there it goes,' Edward heard Lady Anne say. 'It's time we solved this, Ferdy.' The rest was cut off.

The boys pelted down the stairs and came out into a foyer. This one was a lot busier than the one upstairs, and seemed to be at the centre of the hospital. Hundreds of signposts leading to mysteriously named departments showed the way down a labyrinth; but they looked for one sign only, and that was the Exit. It wasn't hard to merge into the crowd of people bustling around. They left the hospital. It was exquisite for Edward to breathe the clear air again.

They found the car park easily. Guy recognised his father's sports car immediately, and they were soon in the back, looking out towards the hospital entrance, waiting for Ferdinand to appear.

'Do you think he'd let me drive this?' said Edward.

'No *way*!' said Guy. 'He wouldn't let *God* drive this car.'

As they caught their breath the hospital door swung open several times, and eventually Ferdinand came out, walking purposefully.

But behind him were Lady Anne and the Reverend, and they were making straight for the car. Mrs Phipps was floating behind them, a monstrous bat.

'Quick,' said Guy. 'Help me.'

He started to pull at the back seat, and Edward tugged at it too, and they shifted it and pulled it and jigged it until it seemed they couldn't jiggle it any more, and finally it came loose as Ferdinand was approaching, and they dived into the boot and pulled the seat back into position just as he opened the front door of the car.

'Anne, I can assure you, I will not be able to help you, whatever you may offer me. And look, it seems the boys have run off, anyway.'

They sat, hunched up in the boot, Edward's leg stuck in an awkward position beneath him, his elbow feeling as if it were about to break.

Ferdinand got in.

'Thank you, Anne. I'm feeling a lot better. I hope you don't mind, but I've got to go and do something very important now.'

They were so squashed in the boot that Edward felt as if all his bones were going to be shattered. He didn't know if it was because Guy's legs were bent underneath him, or if when Edward shifted his weight from one elbow to another he knocked against the back of the seats, which in any case they hadn't shut properly, but he found himself crushed, and suddenly the weight was too much for his elbow, and he was sprawling across the back, in full view of Lady Anne and the Reverend, peering through the window.

'And who might this be?' said Lady Anne.

Ferdinand didn't stop to answer, but started the engine and put his foot down on the accelerator. As Edward scrambled into a more comfortable position he saw Lady Anne making ineffectual gestures at the car.

'Forcefield,' said Ferdinand. 'Should last a bit. Well, that was cutting it bloody fine.'

Guy pushed Edward aside to climb on to the front seat. They drove quickly. The radio was on full blast. Ferdinand didn't seem to want to talk. His face was set in a grim expression, as if he was thinking hard. They were whizzing through places that Edward recognised – forests and fields that he'd often explored with his brothers and sisters. The names of villages on signposts were ones that he had read all his life, that were scored into his mental map. Their syllables were so friendly to see. It was such a relief to see these places again, after the sterile drabness of the hospital. Edward allowed himself some calm.

After they had been driving for about fifteen minutes, Ferdinand relaxed, and he turned the radio down. He let out a sigh of relief.

'Field's off. But they shouldn't be anywhere near. Well,' he said, turning in his seat to look at Edward, 'you've seen that Lady Anne is a very dangerous person.'

'How do you know her?' asked Guy, with an edge of suspicion in his voice.

Ferdinand paused. His expression did not change. 'I used to work with her.' He tapped his fingers on the steering wheel.

'When was that?' said Guy.

'A long time ago.'

They overtook a car, and the engine revved.

Ferdinand smirked. 'It was fun, in the old days. And then Anne and I . . . we parted.'

'Why? What happened?'

'Stop your questioning,' exclaimed Ferdinand, suddenly and fiercely, and Guy was cowed into silence – a feat Edward had never seen performed before.

It was lucky that they had both fallen silent, because Edward had been gazing intently at both of their faces, and now that a wall had been put up between father and son, he didn't know where to look. So he laid his cheek against the glass of the window.

They were driving past a lay-by. In it was a brown

car that he'd seen before at Oldstone Manor. As they sped by it, Edward saw seated in the front the malevolent Mrs Phipps.

'Ferdinand!' Edward said, fully expecting her to pull out.

'What is it, Pollock?' he said, shortly.

The car did nothing. Edward thought maybe it had been a trick of the light. How could it have been Mrs Phipps? he said to himself.

'It's . . . nothing,' he continued out loud, lamely.

They drove on for a few more minutes, and soon passed another lay-by. In it was a hot dog van, and a few cars. Edward held his breath as they passed it. Sure enough, there was the car, and there was Mrs Phipps, blank-faced, buying a hot dog from the stand . . .

'Er . . . Ferdinand . . .' he said.

'Something bothering you?' said Ferdinand.

'Mrs Phipps – I don't know how she's doing it, but she's ahead of us. Even when we overtake her.'

'Ahead of us?'

'All the time – she's been in the last two lay-bys.'

'Oh dear God,' said Ferdinand, and put his foot down on the accelerator. They drove into a narrow lane, which was more like a green tunnel than a road. They sped round a tight corner and came to a squealing halt. Mrs Phipps's car was blocking the way.

Edward was thrown forward against the front seat. Ferdinand and Guy had their seat belts on.

'Get out, quickly, in case you have to run,' said Ferdinand. 'I'll deal with her.'

Guy climbed out and Edward followed. 'Stay behind the car,' said Ferdinand. They hid themselves, but looked out over the bonnet to see what was going on.

A soft breeze blew on their cheeks. Some birds sang. Far off in the distance, cars zoomed by.

Mrs Phipps was much more like a human being than when she'd been in Edward's hospital room. She was grim and determined, heading towards Ferdinand. Ferdinand stood firm and seemed to be drawing on some sort of power source, because Mrs Phipps hit an invisible barrier. She couldn't get past, and floated up and down the edges of it.

'What on earth is he doing?' said Edward.

'Looks like the same sort of thing he was doing in the hospital,' said Guy. 'Bending the rules, I guess.'

Ferdinand looked as if he wasn't going to last much longer.

'He's weak,' whispered Edward, straightening up, and he saw an expression of horror on Guy's face.

Edward saw a jewel glinting, he smelled rich perfume in his nostrils, he felt expensive cloth on his skin.

Sixteen

dward watched Ferdinand crumple to the ground, as if all the bones had been removed from his body. Guy had disappeared. There was a low muttering in his mind, coming from the Other Book. Again he wished that it could help him. He called for Tristram, but the knight did not answer.

Mrs Phipps stood over Ferdinand, her mouth grinning in ghastly triumph. She laughed, quietly, and Lady Anne joined in. She let go of Edward. He knew there was no point in running. Mrs Phipps was guarding the place like a sinister kite.

'Dear old Pollock,' said Lady Anne. 'I'm truly sorry that it has come to this. I had expected that we'd be able to do things with a minimum of fuss. A word from me to Mr Fraser and you were packed off to the asylum. You see Mr Fraser *trusts* me so much. And you were like a little rat in a science lab – I was *so* looking forward to experimenting on you. My friend Doctor Spawforth had some really *interesting* ideas. What is science, but another branch of magic? Smallwood!' she barked.

Edward noticed for the first time the blustery Reverend Smallwood. Once he would have found his broad, cassocked figure comforting – but now he was filled with a deep sense of hatred.

'Tie up this boy and throw him in the boot. And blindfold him.'

Without questioning her, Smallwood caught Edward by the arm. He found a rope in the boot and, though Edward struggled as much as he could, his skinny twelve-year-old muscles were no match for Smallwood's rugby-playing frame. He tied a purple and yellow spotted handkerchief around his eyes.

Smallwood had more difficulty getting Edward into the boot, but he managed, and once more the world was dark and small. The door shut on him with a clang.

Edward could hear noises outside – bumps, low murmurings, the sound of Ferdinand's car being started up, and driven away. He hoped that Guy had had the time and sense to make himself scarce. He guessed if he hadn't, he'd soon find out. Then he heard more murmurs, and the sound of the car doors being opened and closed, and the thrum of the engine being started up. The car accelerated off.

It was hot and dark, and there was a smell of dog food and earth. Edward's heart was thumping as fast as a hummingbird's wings, his throat was as dry as sandpaper, and his stomach felt as if he'd eaten too much lasagne in Kakophagy.

Edward cursed himself and everything around him. He felt at his bonds. The Reverend had tied him up properly. He struggled with them, but however hard he pulled and pushed, he was unable to loosen them. He kicked against the side of the boot, hoping that he might be able to force the door open, but it was impossible. He groaned in frustration.

After what seemed like an age, the car slowed down and came to a smooth halt. He heard gravel crunching underneath the tyres. It was still pitch-black in the boot. Suddenly he heard a 'click', and light filtered through his blindfold.

'Quickly,' said Lady Anne, and he was lifted out. Edward lay limp, knowing that to fight would be pointless. He thought that maybe he'd even gain some sympathy if Smallwood thought he was ill.

Edward was carried a short distance, up some steps, and he heard the scratchy sound of a key in a lock. He was borne through a door, his head bumping against the frame as he went in, and up some stairs. The Reverend found it hard going, and had to stop twice, dumping him like a sack of potatoes. Eventually he heard the creak of another door, and he was hefted on to bare, dusty floorboards. Smallwood took Edward's blindfold off, and stuffed the handkerchief back into his pocket.

'My dear boy,' he said, holding his arms behind him. 'I *am* sorry about this. But it's necessary, you see.' He turned to go.

As the last steps of the Reverend faded away, Edward was left with nothing but dust and darkness for company. He lay there on the boards, and watched the shadows on the floor grow longer and longer, until he thought that they would swallow him up into their strange world.

He fell in and out of sleep. Sometimes he would see Tristram in the distance, and Edward would call to him, but Tristram did not seem to be able to get to him. He wondered if this had something to do with Lady Anne. Sometimes the door to the attic would be opened and Mrs Phipps would come in and force water and food on him. She would bring a bucket too. Edward hated seeing her flat, wrinkled, expressionless face, with eyes that glowed with malice. The more he saw it, the more he realised that it was almost an inversion of

Lady Anne's, and the thought troubled him.

Mrs Phipps came and went about five times altogether, although he soon lost count. It felt as if he was kept in there for days. It was utterly silent. He started to imagine that he could hear the movements of insects in the wood, leading complicated lives, building odd, hidden civilisations about which humans could never learn. There was nothing else in the attic except some old junk – ancient rackets, and cricket bats, some croquet hoops, a broken television.

Again and again he called to Tristram, to his parents, to Ferdinand, but no one ever came except the horrific Mrs Phipps, whose smell made him feel sick. Not once did she speak. All she did was make that strange, whistling, insect noise, that burned into his mind until it was all he could hear. He felt that he would fossilise where he was, that he would become part of the bare boards, that he would decompose into millions of little creatures and melt into the walls.

Then one day Mrs Phipps pulled him up roughly and led him downstairs into a gracious room. It was wallpapered in blue and white stripes with gilded decorations. Lady Anne was seated in a gilt chair upholstered in a deep blue, and the Reverend Smallwood hung back behind her.

'Now then, my dear Edward. We need your

cooperation. Will you help us, Edward?'

'No.' His voice was rusty, low, and it was hard for him to spit out the syllable.

'Fool!' said Lady Anne, and Mrs Phipps gave him a stinging slap on the cheek.

'Never,' said Edward, in a quiet but strong voice.

Smallwood drew towards Lady Anne and, as they muttered together, Edward took the opportunity to look around the room they were in. It was graceful and well-proportioned. Elegant chaises longues and high-backed chairs were arranged around a white marble fireplace, on which stood many invitation cards. Comfortable sofas and armchairs were placed around the edges of the room.

There were portraits on the walls, all sharing char-acteristics of face and bearing. There were shelves of books in the alcoves – Edward couldn't see the titles but they were all uniformly bound and the spines were stamped with a large golden bird. It was the same bird as the crest on the tomb of Tristram de la Zouche. Edward knew that it was a raven. Then realisation dawned. He must be in Lady Anne's house.

Smallwood and Lady Anne stopped their murmur-ings. Lady Anne swivelled towards him, crossing her long, elegant legs, sitting on the deep-blue chair like a queen in judgment.

'If you won't cooperate, then I'll just have to keep you until you do. Take him back up.'

Phipps slithered towards him, and led Edward back up to the attic, slamming the door on him.

Later on, he woke up from a dreamless sleep feeling drained and hungry. Dawn was starting to seep through the tiny window, and he could hear birds singing. Despair was filling his brain, and he could feel the Other Book, whose presence had been largely absent, beginning to make itself known again. Edward cursed it.

'If I were you I would not do that,' said a voice.

Edward spun round on to his other side. Sitting behind him on an old trunk was Tristram de la Zouche, his gilded armour a little faded, his helmet by his side. He was playing with his sword, which was sheathed in its scabbard. Edward was so pleased to see him that his despair vanished instantly.

'Tristram! But why shouldn't I curse the Other Book? If it wasn't for the stupid thing, I'd never've been here, and I'd still be in lessons doing normal things like I expect Strangore is doing now, and I wonder if they've even noticed that I've gone, and if my parents knew I was here I bet they'd rescue me, and I'll never be able to get it back to its owner, if I even knew who that was –'

'Calm, my friend,' said Tristram. 'Soft, soft. The Other Book should not be cursed. I speak as one who knows; for I have a confession that it is meet I make.'

Edward forgot about where he was for the moment. 'What is it, Tristram?'

'It all happened so long ago, and I have been punished for it ever since . . .' Tristram put the sword down. 'You remember those dreams that you had? A boy in Great Hall, and his lunatic father?'

Edward nodded. Some distant images were becoming sharper, negatives developed in the darkroom.

'You remember the book that appeared in that dream? The book which the boy buries, far from sight?'

'Yes,' said Edward. It was clearer now. He could remember . . . the crackling fireplace . . . 'There were two dogs, and they were called . . .' And Edward realised. 'It was you? The boy in the dream?'

'Blanche and Fairfax. Sweet Blanche, and dear old Fairfax. They stayed with me to the end, you know . . .' Tristram looked at the floor and said softly, 'Yes. It was my father who poisoned the Other Book. It is I who have been wandering the worlds of ghosts and shadow-casting men, until the time comes when I can repair the damage that he did, that has come to terrible fruition in Lady Anne. She who will want to become like my father, she who will want to merge this world with the Other . . . It must not happen. She cannot control the Other World. It will control her, and this world will be chaos.

'I cannot stay long. I could not access the place in your mind. I had to fight my way into your world. All I can tell you is that you must fight for me. Remember the prophecy.'

Edward was seized with a tremendous doubt. 'But what if I can't –'

'You have been a better champion, my boy, than I ever was. I could have stopped them . . . I could have rescued her . . .' Tristram's throat seized up and he looked away.

'Your mother,' said Edward.

'Yes,' he answered. 'She whose memory was for a long time the only thing that kept me happy during those years after she died. They made me watch her hang. And I . . . I did nothing to stop it.'

'Why did . . . why did your father want to see her dead?' asked Edward, as gently as he could.

Tristram said, in a matter-of-fact way that Edward knew was covering up great sadness, 'The villagers had been losing their cattle, and they thought she was a witch. If only they knew that it was my father who had been doing it . . . But they wanted to see someone blamed. Nothing got better after that. My father and the Other Book made everything worse.' He pulled his sword in and out of its scabbard, then took it out fully and looked along its length, before putting it back in again.

'I'm . . . I'm sorry.'

'Do not be sorry, for it is all gone now, and I did find peace and happiness in this world for a time.' Tristram smiled, and Edward saw in his eyes the boy who had stood up to his murderous father. He felt suddenly better.

'So I have to help you, Tristram. That's what it was always about. I'll do anything, I swear.' Courage and strength slipped into Edward's bones.

'It is good that you wish to fight,' he said. 'There will be time enough for that. Now, however, I must leave you. I have one message. *You are closer to home than you think.* Farewell,' he said, and he was gone. For a moment Edward thought he had left his sword behind for him as a weapon but, as he scrabbled for it, it vanished.

He was incredibly lonely then, and dejected. But the courage Tristram had given him remained, and though he lay on the ground for nearly a full five minutes, he soon pulled himself together and sat upright. He had to plot his escape.

He looked around and saw the old cricket bats and tennis rackets in the corner of the attic. He could knock Mrs Phipps out when she came up with his food and run outside. But then what would he do . . . Tristram had said he was closer to home than he thought. He rummaged around a bit more and unearthed some ancient tins of tuna. No use, he thought.

He remembered the room he had been in downstairs. The crests on the books, and the portraits . . . could it be possible that it was the drawing room of the guest house at Oldstone Manor, which was attached to the main house, and into which no boy was ever allowed to go?

The more he thought about it, the more likely it was true. Lady Anne wouldn't want to be far from the centre of her operations, so it wasn't likely that he was in London. And all the de la Zouche furniture and paintings would have belonged to the Manor beforehand. Lady Anne was, as she had said, simply returning *home*.

Edward heard steps on the stairs, and quickly grabbed a cricket bat and lay down with it hidden underneath him.

The door creaked open and, instead of the bat-like Mrs Phipps, in came the back of Reverend Smallwood, struggling with a tray.

'Dear boy, dear boy,' he was muttering, 'poor chap . . . should never have got into this . . . can't *think* what his parents will say . . . dear boy . . . I should have stayed in Middle Temple . . . who needs *that* sort of power, I say . . .'

He backed into the room, and turned round to face Edward.

'Pollock. I *am* sorry about this. Don't worry, we'll get you out of here soon enough. I'm afraid I can't do anything about it. You see . . .' and he lowered his voice to a whisper, '*she* won't let me. Some sort of deal hers was . . . I never should have trusted her . . . promising me access to the Other Book . . .'

He came closer and knelt down to arrange the tray. The Reverend had brought him some real food, arranged nicely on a plate with forks and knives, a napkin, and what looked like a whisky. Edward felt sorry for him.

'Medicinal, you know,' he said. 'Thought it might perk you up.' He gave it to Edward, who drank it down. He'd had whisky before, but there was no water in this. It felt like drinking molten lava, then it settled into a warm glow in his gut.

'This Other Book thing, I mean, really,' said the Reverend conversationally. 'It all seems rather silly to me now, don't you think?'

The whisky was making Edward feel sleepy. The Reverend's voice was coming to him as if from a distance. He murmured something.

'I mean, if you just *helped* Lady Anne, then it would be over in a very short time. It would hardly hurt . . . all it would need is a word from you . . .'

To capitulate . . . it seemed like such a wonderful thing. To give in now, and lose the burden which had taken up residence in his brain, in his body. To be free. To be Edward Pollock again. The Reverend's face loomed large and cheerful.

Edward sat up. He was being tricked. Now was the time for action.

Then he heard footsteps on the stairs. He clutched the cricket bat, but there was no use now. Whoever was coming up would be Mrs Phipps or Lady Anne and would thwart any attack he made on the Reverend.

'Cherry tomato?' said the Reverend, looking up, and then someone came down on his head with a cricket bat.

'Sorry, Reverend,' said a girl's voice, as he swooned and fell sideways, still holding the plate, a trembling smile on his face.

Standing behind him was Mandy, still holding the bat, a highly amused expression on her face. 'Crikey,' she said. 'Thank goodness I don't have to confess to him.'

'How did you get here?' said Edward.

'What, not "thank you"? I did what you asked. I kept an eye on Phipps and Lady Anne. There were four trays going in and only three people in the guest house. I followed Smallwood up and found you. Couldn't you look a bit more pleased?'

Edward looked into her glittering eyes, but somehow all he could do was stammer some stupid words.

'Well, come on, then,' she said. 'I'll go first and clear the way. Follow close behind.' She went out of the door, and Edward slipped out behind her.

They made their way quietly down the stairs, passing two landings, and the large drawing room which Edward had seen earlier. Mandy went into the drawing room and made a thumbs-up sign behind her back. Edward heard her speaking to someone, and carried on walking down.

He came to a larger landing which opened on to the hall; he looked down and saw it was empty. There were two large half-tables at the walls, with enormous vases filled with the most tasteful and well-chosen flowers, blue and white orchids. A mirror almost as big as he was made the hall seem much wider. It was nearly black with age at the edges. The black and white marble squares of the hall looked like a chessboard. He ran down the red-carpeted stairs and burst out of the front door. There were two panes of glass in the door, each with the de la Zouche crest on them.

Edward instantly recognised where he was – at the back of Oldstone Manor, in the small guest-house garden which was next to the churchyard. Mr Fraser was the only person he could think of. He knew that he hadn't believed him last time. But who else was there to turn to? Edward sped through the garden and leapt over the wall into the churchyard.

A raven that was perched on Tristram's tomb cawed as he went past. He waved at it. He dashed into the courtyard and, not bothering to knock, came in upon Mr Fraser.

He was still seated at his computer. His red-topped desk was still covered in piles of papers that seemed to have bred since Edward last saw them, half-open files, books with the pages coming out of them, half-full ashtrays and a can of fizzy drink, no doubt confiscated from an unsuspecting boy. He looked up and his creased face became even more wrinkled with astonishment.

'Pollock! What on earth are you doing here? The hospital didn't phone to say you were coming back.'

'You really wouldn't believe me, sir,' said Edward. He realised he was wearing a jumper over his pyjamas.

'Well, Pollock, I am amazed. And you do look *awful*.

Although I've got *business* to be getting on with, I'd rather see you're all right.' He said the word "business" with distaste.

'We do indeed have important *business*,' said a voice, cool and graceful, and Edward turned to see the shape of Lady Anne, curled in a chair, wearing a white dress printed with red birds.

Edward had to act quickly. 'But something terrible is happening,' he said.

'Oh, Edward, how did the hospital let you escape, I wonder?' said Lady Anne, feigning ignorance.

'Don't listen to her!' said Edward. 'She kidnapped me! She sent me to the hospital. She knew the doctor. She knew he'd try things on me. And then she kept me in her attic!'

Lady Anne looked at Mr Fraser. 'Do you see what I mean?' she said. 'Absolutely *mad*.' She said the second word in a fake whisper, behind her hand, as if she was trying to protect Edward from the knowledge, and this made him hate her even more.

'She did! I escaped from the hospital with Ferdinand Lane Glover –'

'Wait a minute – Ferdy Lane Glover? I thought he was certifiably insane,' said Mr Fraser.

'He's not! Well, he was for a bit, but only because he *thought* he was, but anyway now he's as sane as you

242

are and I need to stop Lady Anne because of her ancestor, she can't get the Other Book because she'll make
everything like Tristram's father did –'

'Slow down now, Edward, please,' said Mr Fraser,
not unkindly. 'Why don't you sit down, and I'll phone
your parents, and we'll have you at home in no time.
That place clearly was no good for you. I didn't like
you going there anyway. I was never sure about
Spawforth's methods. *Decidedly* odd.'

'No! Don't send me home. You can't. I have to stop
Lady Anne!'

Mr Fraser looked at Lady Anne, who shrugged her
elegant shoulders. 'I can't think why he's taken such a
dislike to me,' she said. 'We got on so well in English
lessons – didn't we, Edward? Don't you remember? *Ye
have the book: the charm is written in it . . .*'

Mr Fraser looked sharply at her. 'Edward, sit down.
Have a glass of water. I shall call your parents.' He
poured out some water from a heavy jug on his table
and handed it to Edward. Fraser waited till he had finished it, then he picked up the phone.

'No! You mustn't. Please don't. I can't go home. You
have to believe me. I'm not lying. Why would I?'

'Well, quite frankly, Edward, I'm not sure that you
are *quite* yourself now. I don't pretend to understand
how you've arrived here, dirty and tired, but I find it

hard to believe that Lady Anne had anything to do with it. Your last performance in my study was quite something, and I don't want you to overdo it now.' Mr Fraser's dignified face was solemn, his eyes sad but kind at the same time.

'Thank you, Mr Fraser,' said Lady Anne gently. 'You see, Edward? Everything will be all right.'

There was a knock at the door and, to Edward's immense surprise and joy, Will Strangore, Guy and Ferdinand Lane Glover came in. Edward saw the look of surprise on Lady Anne's face.

Mr Fraser stood up very quickly. 'Ferdy!' he said, and held his arms out, as if he hadn't seen a good friend for ages.

'Hello, Alex,' said Ferdinand. 'It's been a long time.'

There was an awkward silence, as the two men wondered whether they should hug or not, and then they did. They patted each other on the back.

'Ferdy Lane Glover. And I thought you'd gone mad!'

'Well . . . I had, a little bit.'

'Hello, Ferdy,' said Lady Anne.

Ferdinand ignored her.

'What, don't you remember Anne?' Fraser asked Ferdinand. 'The fun that the three of us used to have in that little house on Kingston Road?'

'Of course I remember her,' said Ferdinand coldly.

'But first there is something you need to know. I know this seems strange – but you believed in stranger things when we were at university together.'

'That's true, Ferdy,' said Mr Fraser softly.

'I've brought Will Strangore in here, because he has something to say.'

Will looked shyly around the room, his glasses shining in the light. He looked neat and tidy as always, like the lawyer he was bound to become.

'I . . . I'd just like to say,' he said, his voice growing more confident, 'firstly, that I'm sorry, Edward.' He looked at Edward.

Will held Edward's eyes, waiting for a signal. It took a half-second, whilst emotions coursed around Edward's brain – this friend, who had betrayed him – but then he smiled back, and instantly forgave him for running out. 'And . . . and secondly . . .' he wavered, but caught Edward's eye again and spoke more boldly, 'I want to say that whatever Edward has said is true. I saw the Other Book too. I made it expel Guy and get Mr O'Brien in the pond. Sorry, Guy,' he whispered in an aside.

'This is mass hallucination!' said Lady Anne, although there was a note of uncertainty in her iron voice.

'Ferdinand. Please tell me that this is more than just

a game?' said Mr Fraser. 'I am very worried about Pollock. His head has been filled up with enough rubbish. And now Strangore is succumbing too?'

Ferdinand strode into the middle of the room, and he looked tall and proud and knightly; a far cry from the dishevelled figure in his orange dressing gown, mumbling broken snatches of poetry and madness. His long hair framed his gaunt face, and even the camel on his tie looked regal.

'Alex,' he said. 'You should know. After graduating, Anne and I embarked on a research project to find a book that was rumoured to be held by Anne's family – the de la Zouches. All knowledge of it had disappeared in the late seventeenth century. But it was said to be more than just a book. I helped Anne in her search until . . . until I knew that what she wanted was not what I wanted. I had ideals . . . which she twisted against me.'

'But all this is stuff I thought you'd stopped believing in years ago,' said Mr Fraser, 'like me.' He said the second part quietly.

'Yes – I had to take up a respectable post to keep going. But I always wondered about this Other Book, which Anne wanted so much. And then I realised that she wanted it for her own power, she wanted to twist reality to her own bent. And that was when I . . . went mad. I was overworked, and when Anne found out I knew about her real ambitions, she . . . helped me go mad.'

Lady Anne had remained silent throughout all this. In the pause after Ferdinand stopped speaking, Edward noticed with extraordinary clarity every detail in the room. Lady Anne's queenly fingers clasped tightly in the lap of her bird-print dress; a pencil balancing on a pile of papers, about to fall off. The silence was a velvet muffler, smothering and hot.

The pencil did fall off, and the noise broke the silence. Mr Fraser bent down to pick it up, and placed it carefully on his desk.

'Is this true, Ferdy?' said Mr Fraser.

'Yes,' replied Ferdinand quietly. 'And then I realised something.' He held his hands together in front of him, and bowed slightly. 'I realised that Lady Anne was right.'

Edward was distressed, and shocked. It was as if Ferdinand had thrown a spear into his heart. His last friend, his ally . . . it could not be true.

'I realised that you were right,' said Ferdinand, turning to Lady Anne, 'and that perhaps your way is a better way. And so I have brought you a gift. A gift, to reinstate me in your sight, and to bring us both together as the equals we once were.'

To Edward's horror Ferdinand bent down on one knee. 'I have brought you the boy, Edward Pollock, and within him is the Other Book. With your power and mine joined together, as it should be, we can tear it out of him. And once more Oldstone will be the centre of experiment; once more Oldstone shall rule with the unrestrained power of the Other World at its beck.'

Edward was devastated. Everything had shrunk, all his hopes had shrivelled to this small point where now they were destroyed.

'Rise, Ferdinand Lane Glover,' said Lady Anne, and he got up, and stood by her, and they had pride in their faces and terror in their hearts.

'Wait!' said Lady Anne, and spoke a word; and suddenly Mrs Phipps was there, guarding the doors, and the others had frozen – Guy, Will and Fraser were all standing still and silent like dummies in a shop window. Even their skin had taken on a plasticky sheen. The air was thick, like syrup. 'Now they will not hear us; they cannot bother us,' she said, and smiled her cold, elegant smile at Ferdinand, who smiled back, revealing his long canines.

'This should happen at the proper place,' said Ferdinand. 'The place where it all started.' He took Edward's arm and led him outside. Lady Anne came behind him, slow, lissom, baleful, beautiful. Edward glanced back and saw the others.

'What will happen to them?' asked Edward.

'In a few minutes they will wake up. Phipps will see that they believe we have gone for a short walk. They will remember nothing.'

Ferdinand's grip was tighter on him now.

'I hate you,' Edward said to Ferdinand.

'Little *whelp*,' he hissed into Edward's ear, the word startling him.

Ferdinand was leading Edward down to the pond, where the oak tree was, the sibling of the tree in which Merlin was imprisoned. The sky was almost cloud-free. The school ducks were happily quacking in the pond. Edward was sweating a little. Confused feelings were roaring around his skull.

Ferdinand threw him down into the roots of the oak tree. He felt them press into his back. Lady Anne began speaking what must have been the language of the Other Book – cold, clear and cruel. Edward did not understand the words, and then it felt as if a hook had been implanted right in the middle of his chest; he could hear distant voices shrieking otherworldly cries. The hook was so painful that he was racked with a juddering hurt that scraped on every nerve in his body; he struggled to stand up.

Lady Anne was calling the Other Book out of Edward. She was tearing apart his soul, tearing the Other Book out from his inner self. And Ferdinand joined with her. They stood in a terrible circle above him, their lips moving in unison, the weird dirge-like chant becoming more horrible and more nauseating.

Edward couldn't scream because the pain was so intense; he found a small corner of his mind which wasn't full of the now-clamouring symbols and tried to hide there, but he was torn out. The hook began to pull and he was yanked up, up high, almost right off the ground, his body stretched and stretched. A sickness filled him; in his brain now was pain, pain, everlasting, infernal hurt and horror; and noise, too, and the awful, shadowy creature that Edward had seen before, when he had first opened the Other Book, gloating and shrieking, and he knew now that it was an avatar of Lady Anne. Then the noise and pain stopped and he fell to the ground, limp and exhausted.

There was the Book, in Lady Anne's hands. There it was, full of power and hatred, glory and harm; something that Edward knew now both fed into and off the personality of its owners. And there was Ferdinand Lane Glover, the man Edward had trusted, who had behaved to him as if he were a friend, who had pretended to believe him and to help him; and he was nothing but a shadow too, nothing but a man full of deceit and contempt. The sense of betrayal that Edward felt, as he looked into those once-kind, now burning eyes, was more than he could bear.

Seventeen

ady Anne now looked more like a savage queen than ever. Ferdinand was like some cruel despot of the Middle Ages. Behind them the dark green of the daisy-spotted lawn and the blue of the clear sky seemed fake, childish, as if you could pierce through them with a needle and all the air would come out. Edward held on to the tree behind him and it felt like the only thing alive in the world, because everything else was a shell, hollow, empty. Even as he held it, it seemed as if the air around them was thinning, as if creatures were scraping at the walls of this world.

And now he had no friends, no one to trust, no one who could help or defend him. The scraping was becoming louder.

He remembered the bravery of Tristram, when his father had slaughtered the delegation. He summoned up his own reserves – they were small, but he had nothing to lose. If I could only get it back from Lady Anne, he thought . . . She was cradling the Book in her arms as if it were a baby, almost crooning to it.

'*The Other Book*,' she said, softly. 'Oh, Ferdy, we have it now . . . And all this will be so, so *wonderful*.' She stood lost for a moment in visions, and then said with finality, 'I must prepare the charms.'

Edward sprang up from the tree and ran at her, but she stopped him with one movement of her finger, without even looking at him.

'Oh,' she said. 'I had forgotten. *The boy*. What shall we do with him?'

Ferdinand looked at her. 'Leave him to me,' he said. 'I am sure I can find a *use* for him.'

'Don't you come near me!' Edward said, with as much venom as he could muster.

'And what will you do, little rat?' said Ferdinand. He came closer, and Edward felt the strength that radiated from him.

'I'll do my best to hurt you,' said Edward, and when Ferdinand came nearer he kicked him in the shins, but it didn't seem to have any effect upon him. Ferdinand picked him up by the arm as if he had been a doll. He took both of Edward's shoulders, and looked deep into his eyes.

'Don't worry,' he whispered. The strange thing was, that wasn't what his lips said. What his lips said was, 'You stupid little puppy.'

Edward was suspicious. What was going on? Was this another trick of Lady Anne's? He did not want to think that it was some horrible play on Ferdinand's part.

Again the lips moved. 'I'll make short work of you,' but what Edward heard was, 'Sorry, I had to do it, it would have been more painful otherwise.'

More painful? thought Edward.

'Ferdinand!' said Lady Anne. He let go of Edward. 'I think you had better leave that boy to me. You don't seem to be able to get rid of him.'

'But why should we get rid of him?' said Ferdinand. 'He won't be able to do anything. And you have the Other Book now. Surely that is all that you needed, all that you ever wanted, my dear, darling Anne.' And to Edward's surprise, he took hold of her by the waist, and kissed her, deeply. For a moment the shadow from the tree, the gentle summer breeze and the quiet singing of the birds made them seem like young lovers in the countryside. But then the illusion passed.

'Dear old Ferdy,' she said, pushing him off her. 'But you see he *knows*, and just one person who knows my secret is too many. The others –' she cast an arm backwards to the office – 'will remember nothing but a meeting in which I finalise taking over the Manor. The school will move, they'll all drift away, and Pollock here won't be in our lives either – or theirs.' She grinned at him, wolfishly, poised. 'What should we do with you, my dear, dear boy? I think that the Other World might be a fine place for you. I'll prepare the way now.'

Ferdinand looked horrified, and said, 'Anne, no! The boy has done nothing.'

'Silence!' said Lady Anne. 'He will be the perfect final sacrifice. The raven, the dog and the boy . . . You see, Pollock, it is always the powerful who win. The meek won't inherit the earth.' She started to mutter something which made Edward's skin crawl.

He could hear the chatterings and squealings of the creatures from the Other World. He watched Ferdinand try to stop Lady Anne, but Ferdinand could not go near her. There seemed to be a wall of power around her which nothing could breach; she and the Other Book were a parasitic, symbiotic pair, sucking the life out of each other and replenishing it again.

The muttering was becoming louder now, and more horrifying. Lady Anne was going to prove to be worse than Tristram's father, Wentlake. Much, much worse.

He could feel the chattering creatures tugging at him.

They were pulling him out of this world. This really was it. His brain nearly shut down, but he forced himself to stay conscious. He didn't want to meet his first minutes in the Other World unable to defend himself.

However much he fought against the tendrils that scratched at him, they tangled him up the more, until it felt as if he were completely enveloped in a mass of writhing creatures. He was nearly sick, there and then.

Edward was nearing oblivion. He could feel the real world getting fainter and fainter. He said goodbye to his parents, to Ferdinand, whom he saw standing speechless. He gritted his teeth and prepared himself. If Tristram had done it, then so could he. That was how he would repay him – by being as brave as he was. Maybe he could then walk free, if I took his place, he thought. Finally Edward called to his parents, one last, low call, that said to them, I love you, and I will miss you. He felt that call would spread across time and space, and they would hear it and know that he loved them.

Then he heard something soft, yet insistent; something that seemed to call from the depths of someone's soul. And then the real world began to get firmer again, and he saw Lady Anne standing with the Other Book. Edward was filled with a new strength.

There was a puzzled expression on her face – the

first time he had seen her so. She leafed through the Other Book. 'That's impossible. I'm sure I said the spell properly,' she said. She repeated some harsh phrases, and for a moment Edward felt that he was falling back again. But he fought against it, and the figure of Lady Anne became stronger and sharper, and the sky behind her seemed more real too, no longer as if it were a child's balloon that could be burst. He pulled against the creatures that entwined him. And he called again, the call to his parents, that call that all mothers and fathers know, which joins families in iron bonds. And he felt the call stretch so that it was the call of every child to every parent, every nightmare needing to be soothed, every hunger needing to be sated, every harm needing to be healed. And he saw a change come across the faces of Lady Anne and Ferdinand, and he began to understand.

And then he saw Guy running down to the pond, his feet leaving imprints in the long, wavy grass, his face perplexed, to join his father. He noticed the resemblance between the two of them, an odd thing to see when you are on the brink of death. But wheels were clicking in his mind, connections forming, and he managed to stand up. *The line of the wizard and witch is strong*, thought Edward. *I can see them. I can see what is strong*.

'What's going on?' said Lady Anne, confused.

'Guy,' said Edward, croaking in his weakened state.

'What is he saying?' said Lady Anne.

'Guy . . . listen to me. Take it from her.'

Guy hesitated, looked at the boy on the brink of destruction and, without really thinking, launched himself at Lady Anne, and wrenched at the Other Book, and too late Lady Anne realised what was happening and found herself unable to hold on to it.

When Guy took hold of it, he felt a rush of power. He saw a line of people stretching across the centuries, until it came down to him . . . and the one before him he recognised. He felt their wisdom engulf him like a wave.

'I feel it,' he said. 'I know this . . .' He looked at Lady Anne, strangely. Her face . . . distant memories drew together.

A glittering, cold, harsh sound, like a hundred mirrors breaking, resonated; there was a feeling of suspension, as if everything in the world had been put on hold. A gash formed in the air.

Out of it a strange figure approached. The gash closed.

The figure was wearing a tunic, and a lace collar, and breeches. Edward recognised him immediately.

He was the melancholy fellow in the portrait hidden

near the beams of Great Hall, forever looking down upon the father who had cursed him. He was Tristram de la Zouche. He spoke softly to Edward.

'You have nearly completed your task, my faithful squire.'

A sob came from Lady Anne, and everybody turned to look at her.

'Oh, Ferdy,' said Lady Anne. 'I tried to get rid of him . . . I even used Strangore to get him suspended, here, by the pond . . . I knew that he would get in the way . . .' Her long fingers trembled. There were no birds singing now.

She moved towards Guy, and laid her fingers gently on his head. He pulled away.

'My son . . .' she whispered. 'My son . . . Guy . . . my son . . .'

Ferdinand looked as if he wanted to stop her. 'Don't!'

'No,' said Lady Anne, 'he must know now.' She took Guy by the shoulders.

She knelt down in front of him, on the grass, careless of her dress now, her rings flashing quietly in the sunlight. 'Guy . . . my sweet Guy . . . you must understand. There are many things that you have to know, many things that you must learn, and the first of these is that . . . you are my son,' she said, and released him. Guy

259

shrank back to the tree, and looked at his father with something like hatred.

'There is one more thing to be done,' said Tristram, 'before the Other Book can be restored.'

'I know what it is,' said Edward, for in the rushing of his mind there had surfaced one bright thought, as sharp and pointed as steel.

The blood of a maiden.

'*The blood of a maiden must surely be spilled for the source of evil to be truly killed.*' The words of the prophecy felt like fire on his tongue. He sensed fulfilment ahead of him, just in his reach. He turned to Tristram. 'It's Galahad, isn't it? Galahad, the maiden knight. It's me. I'm Galahad. I'm the one who has to be sacrificed. I'm the pure one who has to be sacrificed to get rid of the evil.'

Tristram looked at him and nodded gently. 'Prepare yourself.'

'I'm ready.' Edward braced himself. 'The Other Book, Guy,' he said. 'Hold it out. It is the sacrifice which I must make to purify the evil.'

And before Guy could say anything, Tristram pulled his sword out of his scabbard and ran it into Edward's side. Blood spurted from the jagged wound, on to the Other Book. The droplets were absorbed into its bindings with a sound like water slurping down a plughole.

Pain showered upon Edward, sparking and shivering through his body. There was a shuddering, and a shifting, and he fell to the ground.

A light began to glow from the Book, dim at first, then growing so bright it was impossible to look at. Edward shielded his face, but Guy stood, holding the Other Book in front of him, the light illuminating his face, and there was a roaring sound, the brightness came to a peak, and then there was nothing. Guy dropped the Book.

Tristram spoke, breaking the silence that lay heavy: 'It is purified now. It has been returned. The line of the de la Zouches will flourish once more.'

Lady Anne sat down on the grass.

Edward heard another sound like the first, when Tristram had appeared, but more heartrending still, and three men appeared. They were tall, and Edward thought they looked proud. Though his concentration was ebbing, he saw that they were dressed in long blue tunics, and that they carried weapons which glimmered in the air – part musket, part blade, part something almost organic. As Edward breathed his increasingly more difficult breaths, the air seemed to him sweeter, as if it emanated from the men. They looked to Edward as angels might look – or gods. He spat blood.

'It is finished, my Lord,' said one of them to

Tristram. 'You may go to your rightful place now.'

'Wait,' said the knight, and turned to Edward, who was lying on the ground, the blood still pouring out of him. He welcomed nothingness, void. He was part of everything now, just a mass of atoms, senseless, mindless, without fear, without love, without anything.

He was prepared to die. Tristram had been saved the terrors of the Other World; the Other Book had been restored. The part he had played as carrier and sacrifice was over.

'I give to you my deepest gratitude,' said Tristram. He gave a courtly bow. 'Hold out your hand.' Edward did so, and Tristram held it.

'I'm ready to go,' said Edward. He felt an uplift of power coming from Tristram, so hot it burned. But when Tristram released his hand, Edward felt his vision clear, and the world around him humming with life. The wound in his side was healed. All pain had gone.

Edward felt a cold object in his hand. He opened it and looked down.

'This is my gift to you. It has its own properties,' said Tristram. 'It is the Jewel of the Scryer. Now that Guy has the Other Book, he will need a companion. You have held the Other Book and know what it is. With this, if you wish it, you can aid him in his travails.'

Rage and relief roared around Edward's mind, as he

took the jewel in his hands. It was an emerald, glistening and green, on a thin gold chain.

'What is it?'

'Its uses you shall come to know soon enough,' said Tristram.

A thought struck Edward. 'But why couldn't you have given the Other Book to Guy?'

'He would have been too easily corrupted by Lady Anne. Now it is with him, she cannot take it from him. You could overcome those temptations to power that others could not have. Consider Lady Anne.' Edward looked at her now, seated on the grass, her head still up, but the fire out of her eyes.

Tristram took his sword out of his sheath.

'Kneel, Edward,' he said, and Edward knelt before Tristram. The knight touched him on both of his shoulders with the sword, and said gently, 'You are no longer a squire. Rise, Sir Edward. You are a Companion of the Order of the Blood.'

Edward rose, unsteadily, his heart spilling over with pride, joy, confused and muddled up with fear and foreboding.

'It is time to go,' said one of the men. 'The Other Book will go to the heir of the line.' He picked up the Other Book. It was gloating, strange and alive. And Edward still, slightly, wanted it.

The man spoke formally to Guy: 'You are the son of Lady Anne de la Zouche, you are the next in descent from the Lord Merlin and the Lady Vivien. All hail the new Guardian!' He and the other two men knelt in front of him.

And Guy, who had felt something fresh and wonderful, old and powerful, when he held the Other Book, did not blanch.

Ferdinand looked at Guy and said, 'I will do all I can to help you, Guy. I have so many things to talk about with you.'

Guy looked at the Other Book for a few seconds, and then at his father, who nodded almost imperceptibly. He breathed deeply, and took it from the man's outstretched hands.

'Do you know what the Other Book is?' said the first man.

Guy shook his head.

'It is the repository of Merlin's wisdom, and of Vivien's charms: the words that were said at the beginning and those that will be said at the end of the world. You are the Guardian, you are in it and of it, you will use it and keep it for the rest of your life. You will defend this world against the Other World. You are Lord Guy de la Zouche, Scion of the Blood.'

Guy looked much older, tall and noble. 'I will. I am

Lord Guy de la Zouche, Scion of the Blood,' he said, and his voice was rich with deep music.

The three men bowed low to him. Edward found himself standing up, and bowing too.

'And now, we must deal with Lady Anne, traitor to the line,' said one of the men. 'What happened to Wentlake will happen to you. You wanted to become like him, and so you will.'

They began to fill the air with a strange red light – the light that Edward remembered from his dream, which felt sweet, and good, and yet terrible. It had an odd effect on Tristram. He knelt down and closed his eyes. It looked as if he was crying, or praying.

The red light grew stronger. Lady Anne began to scream, as her poisonous ancestor had screamed so long ago; and then Guy began to shout too, and Lady Anne seemed to be folding in on herself, and Guy cried, 'No!' and ran at the men. Something happened: a battle of wills, a shifting of power; it was as if Guy had taken hold of the light and was pushing it back towards the men. He himself didn't look as if he knew what he was doing; but he began to take control, and the red light faded, and Lady Anne was left crumpled on the grass, her hair spread out beneath her like a carpet on the daisies.

'You can't do it,' said Guy. 'She's . . . she's my mother.'

The men talked angrily amongst themselves. After a while the first man spoke: 'We cannot go against your word, my Lord,' he said. 'But you will pay for it soon enough. Do you accept the condition, or will you see to her punishment?'

And then Edward realised that things are not always closed; that there are gaps through which tragedy slides, that there will always be horror seeping in from somewhere.

'Fine,' said Guy. 'I accept. Save her. I don't care what happens to me.' He did not look at Lady Anne, but she looked at the grass, and wept.

'Thank you, my son,' she said. And Guy went to her, and she sat up, and held him, and they did not speak, and no one knew what went between them.

Tristram went to the men. He was laughing for the first time that Edward had ever seen. His kind, gentle face was lit up in the summer sunlight. The three men bowed to him.

'You are welcome, my Lord Tristram,' said the first of the men.

'It has been a long time,' he said. 'But now I can be at peace.'

He looked back at Edward one last time, and then he and the men vanished.

In the still silence, Lady Anne and Guy got up.

Edward wanted to say something, but he felt that speaking would taint the air.

He walked slowly with Ferdinand, and ahead of them Guy and Lady Anne went, leaning slightly into each other, back up the lawn to the office.

'Hey, Pollock!' said Munro. 'Where have you been? You've really been missing out on things!'

'Yeah, the wierdest thing just happened,' said Peake.

Edward smiled at them. 'Tell me all about it,' he said, and joined them on the way to the dorms.

'Forester fed Page so many carrots his skin went orange!'

Edward laughed; but inside him there welled an enormous feeling of emptiness; it was as if the pain of thousands of centuries was rumbling inside him; the constant presence of the Other Book had gone, and, like a hostage who grows to love his captor, Edward was aching for it.

Edward was taken home for a week, whilst the scandal raged around him. For a while he was withdrawn; he found it difficult to interact with his family. He avoided reading anything. He could still not quite believe that the Other Book had gone from him. It was like losing his closest friend and worst enemy at one blow.

He lay in his room, wrapped up in a duvet and blankets, in spite of the heat, and Tristram did not visit him once. At the back of his mind Edward knew he would never see him again, but still he hoped. Again and again he would take the emerald out of his pocket, twisting it and turning it with his hands, peering into it from every angle. The Jewel of the Scryer, Tristram had called it, but Edward could not make it see anything.

One hot Sunday, he was taken back to school. He stared out of the window for the entire drive, not saying a word. When they came into the Manor, up the drive, the first person he saw was Guy. 'Thanks,' he whispered to his father, and ran out of the car.

They stood there for a moment, in silence, the events of the past weeks hanging invisible but strong between them. And then Guy spoke. He didn't need to say any words of gratitude, and Edward knew he wouldn't.

'So what do you say?' said Guy. 'Feel like being my squire?'

'Shut up, Guy,' said Edward. 'Or should I say, my Lord?'

'Shut up, Ed. Or should I say, Sir Ed?'

The sun was low on the horizon. Below them the thwack of tennis balls sounded softly.

'So?' said Guy. 'Will you help me?'

Edward looked out across the valley, at the slow

river, at the lush fields, and he struggled with words, the membranes on the surface of feelings that we cannot articulate, the double and triple layers of meaning which haunt everything we say. And all that came out, from the massing rush of emotion, were two simple sounds that were to seal his fate for ever: 'I will.'

Acknowledgements

To Lizzie Spratt, Lucy Holden, Georgia Murray and everyone at Bloomsbury. A special mention goes to Lucy Howkins, for taking an interest in my book one wet fireworks night in Dorset – and thanks to Jo Langham for throwing that party. My agent, Felicity Rubinstein. Emma, Andrew, Rose, Helena and Laura Sutcliffe, for lending me the dog kennels at Kildale, and especially Helena for her thoughtful reading. Con and Nicky Normanby, and Sib, Tom and John, for their help and friendship. Alastair Bruton and Fernanda Eberstadt, and their children Maud and Theo, for idyllic summers at Margès. To Nancy Sladek for her kindness in giving me writing days. To Camilla Swift, for my first 'literary' job. To Kira Jolliffe, for publishing my first article in *Cheap Date* when I was still at school. To Bobby Christie, for telling me the first draft of *The Other Book* wasn't the *best* thing I'd ever written. To Alida Christie, for initial proofreading. To Julia

Finch, who marked the first draft like a teacher with a big red pen in a pub in Lyon, and to Olivia Breese for continued support in the line of fire. To Cressida Pollock, for her perceptive comments. To Al Braithwaite for his elegant website. Thanks are due to everyone on whom I forced one draft or another: in no particular order, Katerina Vittozzi, Sibylla Phipps, Iain Hollingshead, Nenna Eberstadt, Ali Price, Kitty Stirling, Marcus Sedgwick, Emma Way, Anna Arco, Lottie Edge, Tom Fleming, Tom Scrope, Lucy McMillan-Scott, Julie Sturgeon, Olivia Cole, Laura Bishop. And finally, to everyone who kept me sane at law school, where I began to write it: Fred Powles, Isobel James, Alex Schofield, Gallia McDermott, Anouska Spiers, Max Neuberger and Charlie Flodin.